KARMA KHULLAR'S
mustache

KARMA KHULLAR'S mustache

KRISTI WIENTGE

Simon & Schuster Books for Young Readers
NEW YORK   LONDON   TORONTO   SYDNEY   NEW DELHI

SIMON & SCHUSTER BOOKS FOR YOUNG READERS
An imprint of Simon & Schuster Children's Publishing Division
1230 Avenue of the Americas, New York, New York 10020
This book is a work of fiction. Any references to historical events, real people, or real places are used fictitiously. Other names, characters, places, and events are products of the author's imagination, and any resemblance to actual events or places or persons, living or dead, is entirely coincidental.
Text copyright © 2017 by Kristine Wientge
Cover illustrations copyright © 2017 by Serge Bloch
Cover photograph of mustache
copyright © 2017 by DutchScenery/Thinkstock
All rights reserved, including the right of
reproduction in whole or in part in any form.
SIMON & SCHUSTER BOOKS FOR YOUNG READERS
is a trademark of Simon & Schuster, Inc.
For information about special discounts for bulk purchases,
please contact Simon & Schuster Special Sales
at 1-866-506-1949 or business@simonandschuster.com.
The Simon & Schuster Speakers Bureau can bring authors to your live event.
For more information or to book an event, contact the Simon & Schuster Speakers
Bureau at 1-866-248-3049 or visit our website at www.simonspeakers.com.
Also available in a Simon & Schuster Books
for Young Readers hardcover edition
Interior design by Hilary Zarycky
Cover design by Lizzy Bromley
The text for this book was set in ITC New Baskerville.
Manufactured in the United States of America
0820 OFF
First Simon & Schuster Books for Young Readers
paperback edition August 2018
4 6 8 10 9 7 5 3
The Library of Congress has cataloged the hardcover edition as follows:
Names: Wientge, Kristi, author.
Title: Karma Khullar's mustache / Kristi Wientge.
Description: First edition. | New York : Simon & Schuster Books for Young Readers, [2017] | Summary: "A biracial Indian/Caucasian girl is nervous to begin middle school, especially since her mother is now the breadwinner of the family, her best friend may no longer be a bestie, and the appearance of the seventeen hairs over her lip that form a very unwanted mustache" —Provided by publisher.
Identifiers: LCCN 2016024635 | ISBN 9781481477703 (hardcover) | ISBN 9781481477710 (pbk) | ISBN 9781481477727 (eBook)
Subjects: | CYAC: Middle schools—Fiction. | Schools—Fiction. | Best friends— Fiction. | Friendship—Fiction. | Racially mixed people—Fiction. | East Indian Americans—Fiction. | Mustaches—Fiction.
Classification: LCC PZ7.1.W492 Kar 2017 | DDC [Fic]—dc23
LC record available at https://lccn.loc.gov/2016024635

To my parents, who always believed I could

KARMA KHULLAR'S mustache

Chapter One

Dadima used to say I'd be as strong as a lion if I drank milk twice a day. She never mentioned I'd get as hairy as one too. There should have been a disclaimer—bold letters and a voice-over with a list of side effects scrolling along the side of my grandma's face whenever she handed me a cup of hot milk.

Daddy's back was to me as he pried paratha dough off the rolling pin in a misshapen glob. The orange ties of his *Karma Is Served* apron clashed with the pale green of his turban. He loved that he'd found an apron with my name on it, but whenever he reminded me for the hundredth time that he was wearing my name, I had the urge to accidentally spill curry down the front of the apron.

Once he had the paratha on the smoking pan, I tipped the milk he'd poured for me into a potted plant next to me.

This entire summer the universe had been against me. The hair on my face just happened to be the most recent tragedy. The worst part was, I didn't know how to get rid of it.

Luckily for me, my best friend, Sara—a walking, talking guide to fashion and personality quizzes—had returned from vacation. She'd just called to figure out what time I should be at her house that afternoon to compare notes on our class placement lists, which had just arrived in the mail. Thank Babaji we were in the same block.

Daddy flipped the paratha and turned to me. "Just like Dadima's," he said, grinning. "Am I right, *beta*?"

The almost-burned smell of Daddy's parathas on the roti pan that Dadima'd brought from India stirred a lump behind my heart, which I quickly tried to ignore. Parathas hadn't been the same since Dadima had died last summer.

I cupped my hand over the mouthpiece of the phone when Daddy turned back to the stove. "I'm serious, Sara. There are exactly seven*teen* of them." I

2

pinched the hairs above my lip, hoping no more had grown. I didn't want to show up at orientation with a mustache, even if Sara would be there at my side.

"Mmm-hmm." Sara's breath rattled through the phone.

I pictured her blowing a loose strand of hair out of her eyes.

This was the second time I'd brought up my mustache to her. She wasn't paying attention. *Again.*

Daddy pushed a hot paratha across the counter to me. It wasn't exactly square-shaped like Dadima's used to be, but anything tasted better than Mom's freezer-burned casseroles. He reached across the counter and held out the carton of milk. I slid my hand over the mug and shook my head.

"What about being strong—" Daddy started to say.

"As a lion?" I went to the fridge and grabbed the orange juice.

Overdosing on milk probably hadn't given me my mustache, but Daddy had stopped buying organic now that he was a stay-at-home dad. I'd overheard Mom tell him that the hormones in non-organic milk weren't good for girls. So, for the past two weeks I'd been dumping my milk into the nearest potted plant whenever Daddy wasn't looking.

"What about lions?" Sara asked.

"Nothing," I said as I poured my juice. Then I lowered my voice, even though Daddy was humming a Bollywood tune and most likely daydreaming he was the star, and not really paying attention to my conversation. "Well . . . don't you think it's odd? Maybe a hormonal imbalance or a gene mutation, or maybe I'm turning into—"

"Oh. My. Gosh! Please don't say what I think you're about to say."

"What?"

"A werewolf."

My breath stuck in my throat. I needed to swallow, but something was in the way—my heart. "I was going to say 'a boy.'"

Sara hadn't said "werewolf" as an insult, but now that the idea had been verbalized, it was free to run wild. It existed now. I could imagine the boys at school saying it with smirks on their faces. Friday. At orientation, ruining the school year before I even had a chance to make my own first impression.

"Oh." Sara let out another sigh, but this one was a softer, *I'm sorry* kind that sounded more like the Sara from the beginning of summer, who I could tell anything to, and less like the Sara who ignored me. "Look, we'll talk about it when you come over later. Okay?"

"Yeah, okay. See ya later." I tore off a piece of paratha and dabbed it into the stream of melted butter that ran through the middle of the rhombus-shaped bread.

"Watch this, *beta*," Daddy said, trying his hand at tossing another paratha into the pan with a flip of his wrist.

He'd definitely watched too many cooking shows recently.

I finished breakfast as quickly as possible. The phone call with Sara left me shaky. She'd only been on vacation for two weeks, but the space between us that had always been pulled together like we were two attracting magnets now felt like it was pushing us apart, as if her pole had flipped. Once I saw her, it'd probably all go back to normal. I mean, she did only come back last night, and it *was* a long drive from her cousin's house in South Carolina.

"Thanks, Daddy." I kissed him on the cheek and rushed upstairs to claim the bathroom before Kiran.

Once I'd locked the door, I leaned close to the mirror to get a good look at my face. I counted again. Yep. Seventeen. Seventeen hairs on either side of my upper lip.

How many hairs made a mustache? At least twenty? I hoped it was at least twenty. Fifty or a hundred would be perfect. The further away I was from having a real-life mustache, the better. Best of all would be finding a way to get rid of it, especially before school started.

The hairs around my mouth were dark enough that each strand was visible. When I stretched the skin, I could pinpoint each pore that a hair grew out of, the way grass sprouted out of a sandbox.

My Horrible Histories books mentioned that ancient monks rubbed stones on their heads to make themselves bald. After reading that a couple of weeks ago, I started to rub the sides of my mouth in circles with my finger, in the hopes that the motion would work for my face. It wasn't exactly scientific, but it was the only thing I had, considering Mom didn't own a single pair of tweezers and she drew in her barely-there-blond eyebrows every morning, and Sara hadn't been very helpful on the phone. But all that the rubbing had done was make the sides of my mouth red and chapped.

I turned the water on to cover up my ritual. I

knew it was silly, but at least everyone would think I'd brushed my teeth really well.

"Hurry up!" Kiran yelled, banging on the door.

I squirted toothpaste into my mouth and swished some water around. I also ran my toothbrush under the water so it looked like I'd brushed properly.

Kiran stood outside the door when I opened it. His black hair stuck out at random places, and his breath stunk worse than the tennis shoes he'd been mowing in all summer.

"You forgot to shave," he said, and pinched the hair at the edges of my mouth.

It annoyed me that he knew what I'd been doing, even though I'd left the water running. "Stop it, jerk." I swatted his hand away.

He was fourteen and probably *wanted* a mustache, so why was *I* the one with hair on my face?

Chapter Two

A woman's shrill voice blasted through the speakers as Daddy started the car. I buckled my seat belt in the backseat, knowing exactly what he was going to say during the car ride. I could even make a mental checklist of his questions and annoying comments and put ticks next to them in my head once they'd been said. Sometimes I did.

"She has the voice of a bird." Daddy smiled at me in the rearview mirror.

Annoying comment number one, *tick*. I imagined a bird being strangled, because that's how Bollywood music sounded to me.

"*Main dhoondoo bichhade yaar ko,*" blared out of the speakers as we drove toward the main road that led across town to Sara's house.

Shriveled cornfields blanketed the ground on either side of the road. Way back beyond the field was the University of Creekview. I tried not to stare as we drove closer to where the top of the steeple from the University of Creekview's chapel poked above the tree line—even though it was my favorite view in the entire town—because mentioning the university made Daddy pull his beard and breathe in and out of his nose.

"Do you know what she's singing, *beta?*" Daddy asked, drumming the steering wheel with his hands to the beat of the Bollywood music.

Tick. Whenever Daddy heard a Bollywood song, that question always followed.

"*Hanji,* Daddy." I nodded. Even though he knew I understood, he'd still translate.

"I'm searching for my lost love."

Tick, annoying comment number three.

I silently chanted *Satnam Waheguru* over and over until I cleared my head of any negative thoughts. I'm only half Sikh—the other half of me is Methodist—but Dadima used to tell me to chant this when I felt myself getting annoyed.

I loved Daddy, but now that he was a stay-at-home dad, his repetitive questions and mood swings crawled under my skin and made me itch the same way I did when I heard someone talk about bedbugs. Even Kiran had walked to his mowing job instead of letting Daddy drive him. And Kiran hated walking. And working outside, for that matter. The only reason he went was because he got paid for it and he was saving up for a phone.

We passed the grocery store and the new high school, driving into the part of town where the houses were bigger and newer than in my neighborhood. Daddy drove the car through the short, winding streets that were named after different types of birds, like Falcon Drive and Cardinal Crescent. Sara's subdivision had been a big field until two years ago but was now filled with rows and rows of almost identical-looking houses.

As we turned left onto Sara's road, the first thing I saw was a moving van parked across the street from Sara's.

In front of my house!

Okay, so it wasn't technically my house.

Sara and I had made plans that my family would move there. It had been a pretty hopeless idea then, and was even more so now that Daddy had lost his job. Still, it took several *Satnam Waheguru*s to stifle the pang of jealousy that squeezed my chest. I had known that someone would move into that house, and I had known it wouldn't be me, but it didn't make the sight of that moving van any easier.

Living across the street from Sara was one of the many things I liked to pretend could really happen. The same way I liked to imagine my mustache might disappear if I stopped thinking about it for long enough. Half nervous habit and half wishful hoping, I patted at my upper lip. The fuzz at the edges of my mouth was still there.

When I'd first noticed my facial hair a week ago, I'd waited for someone to be like, "Hey, what's that on your face?" If anyone had seen, they hadn't said anything—except for Kiran, but brothers don't count. Then again, it was summer. The only people I saw regularly were Sara, her family, and a few kids at the pool, and Sara'd been away for two weeks.

Daddy tapped the car window with his finger toward the house.

"Houses are a big investment. What ever happened to investing in the mind? Am I right, *beta*?"

Double *tick*.

"*Hanji*, Daddy." If I agreed, he'd stop before the ranting really began. The one that went, "Khullars have always been frugal spenders with brilliant minds. Babaji tells us in the great word . . ." And by "frugal" Daddy meant "cheap."

I'd definitely inherited that trait from him. I couldn't waste a thing and wore my clothes until Mom threw them out and made me shop for new ones. It's not that I didn't care how I looked. I just grew really attached to my favorite T-shirts and things. Spending money on new clothes I'd have to break in until they stopped being itchy didn't really make sense to me when I had so many comfy clothes I liked. Mom had been too busy this summer to pay much attention to my ratty T-shirts and too-small shoes. She'd die if she saw how far my toes dangled over the front of my silver strappy sandals.

Daddy stopped the car in Sara's driveway. He got out and opened my door. I cringed as it made a loud groan before slamming shut.

"I'll have that fixed by the weekend," Daddy said.

I stared up at Sara's house. My stomach did this kind of water balloon flip-flop when I saw Mrs. Green weeding the flower boxes on the front porch. It reminded me of how my life used to be. Over the summer the flower boxes on our porch had been replaced with recycling containers. Daddy didn't have much of a green thumb and Mom was too busy, so the withered plants got thrown away and Kiran put the recycling on the porch because he's too chicken to go into the garage at night. Not that he'd ever admit that.

"Hello, Karma. Dr. K." Mrs. Green had a smile that made you go as gooey and warm as the middle of a chocolate chip cookie right out of the oven. "Sara's in the basement."

"Thanks." I gave Daddy a sideways hug. "See ya later."

I ran inside and down the stairs. All the houses in Sara's neighborhood had a fully carpeted basement with a mini-kitchen. It was our own miniature house when Sara and I were together.

Sara sat on the floor and was taking clothes out of a big, black garbage bag when I got to the bottom of the steps. "Hey, Karma," she said, smiling.

Her younger sister, Ruthie, bounced over to me with streaks of blue, pink, and green eye shadow caked onto her eyelids.

"You look just like Fancy Nancy," I said, grabbing Ruthie under her arms and spinning her in a circle.

Ruthie threw her head back and giggled. "Wanna makeover?" She grabbed my arm and pulled me toward the corner where her toys and plastic play kitchen were.

"Ruthie, that's not the kind of makeover Karma needs."

So, I *did* need a makeover? A flash of embarrassment seared my cheeks. Maybe at least one good thing would come out of her new magazine obsession: helping me figure out a way to get rid of my mustache.

Once upon a time I'd been the one with the ideas, but this problem was way out of my expertise. I guess Sara had listened to me earlier. I pushed that squirminess of doubt I'd felt this morning on the phone way down to where I hoped it'd disappear.

Sara grabbed my other arm and pulled me down next to her on the floor. Something about her hair looked different, smoother than usual. Her lips were shiny, and I might have caught a hint of sparkle just above her eyes.

I tried to send a sorry-shrug to Ruthie, but she'd already made it halfway up the stairs, yelling for a snack.

"What's all this?" I asked, taking in the piles of

clothes littering the floor around Sara but still trying to see anything else new or different about Sara out of the corner of my eye.

"My cousin Rachel's clothes. They're in really good shape. She told me she outgrew some of it really fast last year and only wore them a couple of times. She's practically five nine. Not tall enough to model on the runway, but she could totally do magazines. I mean, look at this stuff," Sara said, pushing a simple dark blue shirt close to my face. "She's got the best style sense ever."

Sara grabbed another shirt from the pile and held it up to her chest. "This is going to be perfect for a first-day-of-school outfit. *Teen Bop* said that thrift finds are what's in for fall." She stood up and studied herself from several angles in the full-length mirror. "Why don't you pick some shirts and shorts? There's even a few pairs of sandals in there. We need a good orientation outfit for Friday and one for the first day of school."

If it hadn't been for Sara and me always sharing clothes, I might have been offended at her telling me to take her cousin's clothes. Sara knew about Daddy's job, but I wondered if maybe offering me free clothes had more to do with her sudden interest in fashion, while I sported my usual "T-shirt chic" look, as I liked to think of it.

I picked up a bright pink shirt from a pile close to me and started to unfold and refold it. The top of the sleeves puckered and bunched over the shoulder. It was a small detail but something that would drive me crazy and make me self-conscious all day if I wore the shirt. Especially with the puckering sleeves being so close to my face. I didn't want to draw attention to my upper lip.

Sara talked about *Teen Bop* and held up different skirts and tops as she swished back and forth in front of the mirror.

"Don't think I haven't noticed you folding and refolding that shirt, Karma." Sara's right eyebrow raised to a point, but her eyes stayed fixed on her reflection in the full-length mirror in front of her. "I just read this article that said the first step to a big change is to make a small change. You know, wear something *daring*. I plan on wearing a skirt on the first day of school. You know how much I hate how skirts ride up when I walk, but we're going to be in the *sixth grade*, Karma. We've got to start taking some chances. It's middle school, for goodness' sakes."

"It's just—" My cheeks burned, partly because Sara had noticed me refolding the shirt and partly because she scared me with all this "taking chances" stuff. I mean, I was all for trying new things, but too many new things were going on right now. Mom at work, Daddy at home, and hair on my face kind of put me over my "new stuff" limit. I didn't need a spotlight on me in middle school, at least not until I figured out how to get rid of my mustache.

"Let me guess." Sara tossed the shorts in her hand onto the floor. "Is this like the time you thought you had a tumor and it turned out to just be your cheekbone?"

I opened my mouth to protest, because the lump had been behind my ear, and it was definitely a weird bump that had no business being there. Sara threw her hand up to shush me.

"Wait! Or that time you kept making me squeeze your elbow because the bone jutted out too much and you insisted your joints were swollen due to a tropical disease Emma had brought back from vacation?"

"You know I had that weird cough and . . ." I knew better than to argue with Sara when she was goofing off. At least I hoped she was still goofing off.

Sara laughed and sat down next to me. I threw a pile of clothes at her, but she caught them and tossed them back at my face.

"Seriously, Karma. You've got to lighten up and stop being so paranoid."

"I'm not paranoid. I'm cautious."

"Well, stop being *cautious.*"

Sara said "cautious" as if it was a bad thing.

When I stayed quiet, Sara sat up and shrugged. She started digging through a stack of skirts next to her. She acted calm, like she'd already forgotten what we'd just talked about, but I saw a few splotches on her neck and knew I'd annoyed her somehow. They were the same splotches Sara got when Ruthie called her Sissy in public.

I reached for some shorts and pretended to care whether or not they would fit me. Really, though, I tried to figure out what had changed between us. It wasn't just today. It'd been happening all summer. Little things. She'd pass me a napkin at the pool and tell me to wipe the chocolate off the sides of my mouth before I'd even had a chance to lick it. Or she'd huff when I didn't know what to say about a song or someone's outfit.

"Rachel told me all about her high school orientation. Did Kiran go to his?" Sara asked.

I nodded.

"Don't you wish we were going into high school instead of only middle school?" Sara let out a long sigh.

Just before she'd left for her vacation two weeks ago, we'd had a long talk about how much we were going to miss elementary school. Neither of us looked forward to going from the oldest in the school to the youngest.

She continued to talk about how big the middle school was and how she couldn't wait to have a real locker, and then started using words like "A-line" and "boho" as she sifted through the stacks of Rachel's things. I let her talk because I didn't mind letting her fill the space between us in the way feathers filled a pillow, in that light and breezy kind of way that gave my brain a break from overthinking everything.

Instead of stressing about how I'd deal with everything middle school, I focused on the fruity smell that drifted from the piles of clothes. Probably the smell of Rachel's bedroom. Probably perfume. I bet everyone in high school wore fruity-smelling stuff. Fake fruit smells gave me a headache.

19

I leaned up with my feet under me, reached into the nearly empty garbage bag, and shook out the last few things. Three bras tumbled onto the floor by my knees.

One had the same shape as a cutoff tank top. The other two were proper bras with wire and the shape of a boob without one even in it.

I grabbed a bra with a boob shape and stood next to Sara in front of the mirror. Then I mimicked the side-to-side swishing she'd been doing with the skirts, but with my chest stuck out.

Sara's neck turned even more splotchy. She snatched the bra out of my hands.

"Jeesh, Karma. That's so immature."

I shrugged, trying to shake off the word "immature." I hated that I'd annoyed Sara again and that I didn't understand why. Sara was the first person I had ever felt comfortable being silly in front of—and I *was* just being silly—but somehow that one word "immature" shifted this and every other time I had tried to be funny. Like how people say their lives flash before their eyes when they die, my entire summer of conversations with Sara flashed before me. Had she seen all my goofing off as immature and not silly the whole time?

Somewhere between our last day at elementary school and the middle of summer, an invisible rulebook had been wedged between us. Sara had read the book, and somehow I was supposed to guess what was inside.

Chapter Three

Thank Babaji for Ruthie. Just as the weird-ness between Sara and me started to charge the air with the same intensity of an electric storm, Ruthie yelled, "Oreos! I've got Oreos!"

She held the blue package over her head as she bumped down the stairs on her butt.

Sara snatched the package from Ruthie at the bottom of the steps. Ruthie tried to snatch them back, but Sara held them over her head.

"You'll break them all," Sara said, pushing Ruthie away and clearing a space on the floor.

We sat where the piles of Rachel's old clothes had been scattered and waited as Sara opened the package of cookies exactly on the red line, so it'd be easy to reseal. It's how she opened everything.

"You're taking forever on purpose, Sissy. I'm telling Mom." Ruthie made a halfhearted lunge for the cookies.

Sara finally passed us each two. She twisted the top off hers and licked the middle before sticking it back together. Her cousin had once told her that was a cure for cancer. Obviously she doesn't really believe that anymore, but she still does the ritual. I smiled and broke off the top black biscuit, chewed it to a mushy pulp, and used my tongue to stick the pulp over one of my front teeth. I knew the whole bra thing had annoyed her, but she'd still laugh at a non-bra joke, right?

"Hey, do I have anything in my teeth?" I asked.

Ruthie laughed so hard, she spit flecks of black, gooey mush onto the carpet and the open bag of cookies.

"Gross." Sara snatched the cookies away from us. "You're spitting all over them." Sara threw a napkin at Ruthie. "Clean your mouth. It's disgusting."

Ruthie stuck out her black-coated tongue before she took a napkin and wiped at her mouth and cheeks.

"Here," Ruthie said, handing me a napkin.

"Thanks, but I don't need one as much as you,"

I said, reaching toward Ruthie to help her wipe her face.

"Yes, you do. It's all over your mouth," she said, laughing.

"It's all over your teeth," I said jokingly back to her.

"No, really, Karma." Ruthie stopped giggling. "It's all in the hair on your mouth."

I flinched as she said it and licked the napkin so I could wipe at my upper lip. My face prickled like a million bee stings on top of a sunburn.

Ruthie had noticed my mustache. I rubbed at my upper lip until the napkin started to shred, but the friction of the napkin on my face was the only thing stopping me from crying. Why the heck did rubbing work for those monks and not for me, when they got to live up in mountains where no one ever saw them? I had to go to school in less than a week. Middle school, where a couple hundred kids, mostly older than me, would definitely notice hair on my face if a five-year-old did.

It was one thing to know I had a mustache but something completely different for Ruthie to say it out loud. Sure, Kiran made fun of me all the time for any reason whatsoever, but I wasn't used to someone I liked mentioning my mustache right to my face.

"Ruthie, take these back upstairs," Sara said, shoving the package of cookies into Ruthie's hands.

"I don't want to. I want to play with you guys."

"We're eleven. We don't *play*. Go upstairs." Sara stood up and pushed Ruthie toward the steps.

I was grateful for Sara getting rid of Ruthie, but it frustrated me that I had to be rescued from a five-year-old.

"Is it really that bad?" I asked. I said it in a whisper because I wanted to know what Sara thought, but I also wanted to pretend that none of it was actually true. Maybe I hadn't heard Ruthie right and I'd been imagining my mustache this entire time.

"What?" Sara asked, digging through a pile of clothes.

All summer Sara had made a huge deal about weird things like the name of the song coming through the speakers at the pool or the color of the nail polish on her toes. Jeesh! Her mom had only just let her wear polish, and she acted like it was such a big deal. I was starting to feel like she didn't care about anything important to me.

"*What?* You know what. My mustache. Even Ruthie noticed it."

"Come on, she's only five. What does she know?" Sara rolled her eyes, but I didn't know if it was because she was trying to pretend that what Ruthie said didn't matter or because I'd taken Ruthie so seriously.

Either way, Sara couldn't just keep trying to brush off this whole issue. If my mustache was something I could easily wipe away like dusting off bread crumbs, duh, I would. Unfortunately, it was more like a glob of mustard that just got worse the more I tried to get rid of it.

"Don't you notice it? I mean, if Ruthie notices it, *everyone* will notice it."

"Jeesh, Karma. Don't be so dramatic. It's no big deal. You only notice it because it's on you."

My teeth clenched together so hard, the inside of my ears tingled. It *was* a big deal. Having a mustache was a huge deal, not only because I was eleven but because I was a girl. Even boys my age got made fun of for having the beginnings of a mustache. I know because last year Ronny Shaw got teased for the scraggly hair that had started to grow at the sides of his mouth and on his chin.

Sara might not have been quite herself this summer, but she was still my best friend, and a best friend should think *my* big deals were *her* big deals too.

Sara reached over and touched my shoulder. "Ruthie notices everything. She's always like that. If my mom moves a picture frame, she says something. It's her most annoying quality—aside from being five."

After a few quiet moments she added, "Listen, we'll read through all my magazines at the pool tomorrow. I'm sure we'll find something to help with the hair, okay? Trust me. No one at orientation will notice it. Plus, we can do a makeover on Friday for our sleepover, okay?"

All my muscles loosened. I even agreed to wear the pink top with puckered sleeves for orientation, and a cotton skirt with tiny swirls of embroidery edged at the bottom seam, for the first day of school.

A new outfit wasn't exactly the permanent fix for my mustache that I'd been looking for, but at least Sara had agreed to help me figure out a plan.

Chapter Four

I squinted as the sun reflected off the million tiny wavelike ripples in the pool water, giving me time to stare at the girl walking next to Sara, without looking like I was staring.

Daddy had dropped me off early, and I'd secured our usual spot under the big tree near the fence that ran along the perimeter of the swimming club's property. I'd never seen this girl before, and Sara hadn't mentioned anything about inviting anyone. But even from across the pool it was obvious the girl had a walk and way about her that screamed, *Hot-water girl.*

Sara and I had come up with our hot-water/cold-water-girl theory in the pool changing rooms last summer. Whoever turned the hot water on in the showers first got the hot shower, and the other shower would be freezing cold. So we both took cold showers, thinking we were letting the other get a hot one. It was only when we both came out with blue lips on an overcast day that we realized we'd both been taking cold showers for weeks. After that, sometimes we'd lie on our towels, peeking over the tops of our books, and divide the girls we saw into the hot-water or cold-water group.

As Sara and whoever she was got closer to the spot where Sara and I always sat, this hot-water girl pushed her sunglasses to the top of her head. Her eyes were ice—a too-light blue. It made the hairs on my arms stand up the way they did when I stepped out of the pool and into a gust of wind. But more than that, her eyes were calm, but not peaceful. Ocean-before-a-hurricane calm. Or at least that's what I'd read. Daddy wasn't really one for splurging on a beach vacation.

"Karma," Sara said when they reached me. "This is Lacy. She's from California!"

California. Big deal. Sara hung on to that word as if the entire world revolved around California. If you ask me, the middle of the Midwest where we stood was closer to the center of the world than a long, skinny state stuck at the edge of the country like an afterthought. Come on. If the world sneezed, the entire state would break off and drift right into the ocean.

"Lacy, this is Karma." Sara smiled at us both. I could tell she wanted us to smile at each other too.

I nodded at Lacy, careful not to blink. I didn't want to know Lacy with her smooth, blond hair. I didn't even know why Sara wanted to hang out with her. But I could tell from the way Sara's eyes took in Lacy's every hair flick that Lacy would be a part of my life whether I wanted her to or not—at least for today. It wouldn't take Sara long to figure out that Lacy would scrap us for cooler girls the first chance she got. The quicker I could get Sara's focus back on track, the better. Orientation and our sleepover were Friday, and we needed to find a solution for my mustache by then. No way would we discuss my mustache in front of this girl. How could a girl like her even begin to understand a problem like mine?

"She's the one who moved in across the street from me!" Sara said.

We'd watched that moving van yesterday afternoon from Sara's bedroom window after the awkward Oreo incident. All we ended up seeing were boxes and furniture wrapped in plastic. Not enough to figure out who lived there. Now this girl with the icy eyes stood in front of me, hogging all of Sara's attention.

"Karma, you won't believe it, but she's in our class, too!"

Yep. The way my summer had been going, why wouldn't I believe she'd be in our class too?

"Do you always sit here?" Lacy eyed my towel and book under the shade of the only tree. Her head turned toward the pool, most definitely calculating how far away we were from the other kids our age already splashing in the water.

"Well, it's shady," Sara said.

I noticed she didn't say, "It's our favorite spot" or "It's where we always sit." Instead her mouth twisted like she couldn't figure out the flavor, the way she did in the middle of one of our blind taste tests when her dad would go crazy in the ice cream section of the grocery store and come home with five cartons.

"Don't you want to be in the sun?" Lacy asked.

I wanted to explain about the dangers of ultra-violet rays, but Tom and Derek, two boys we'd gone to school with since kindergarten, showed up with a volleyball and started a game right in front of my towel.

Derek said hi. Sara nudged me, so I said hi back even though his eyes were on Lacy the whole time. He'd probably only said hi so Lacy would think he was nice. Tom only came up to Derek's ear, but he bounced around so much, you almost thought they were the same height.

Tom grabbed the ball from Derek and set it up high for Derek to spike. Tom made it so obvious that they were showing off for Lacy. I shook my head, actually glad Lacy didn't want to sit here. I was bending down to get my stuff, when Lacy smiled and put her things down on the grass.

"Now I know why you sit here. Nice view."

Lacy took off her cover-up, which happened to be a dress. She had on a pink bikini, and the top didn't look saggy or stuffed either.

Sara cough-laughed the way she did when Ruthie asked her to play Barbies in front of anyone other than me. But the fact that Lacy was making herself comfortable made Sara relax and pull off her T-shirt and shorts too.

She didn't have on the usual one-piece she'd worn all summer. Her new suit was a two-piece. The top had more shape than I thought Sara really had. I looked down at my black-and-purple Speedo.

The volleyball hit the ground near our towels.

"Eye on the ball," Derek said, laughing.

Tom threw the ball at Derek, and they started wrestling.

I shook my head, but Sara and Lacy giggled. It made me wish Lacy had never come to Creekview, Ohio, so Sara would go back to normal-Sara, who wore a Speedo and rolled her eyes along with me before putting her nose right back into a magazine.

"Who are they?" Lacy asked.

"The cute one is Derek. The dopey one is Tom," Sara said.

"Cute?" I asked.

"Sure." Sara shrugged, but her hand reached up to rub her neck.

"He's totally cute," Lacy said, nudging Sara and giving me a slow blink that reminded me of how Ruthie closes her eyes when she doesn't want to listen. It's the kind of blink that says, *It's better when I can't see you. So why don't you just disappear?*

"Speaking of cute." Sara pulled a stack of magazines out of her bag.

Lacy grabbed one off the top of the pile. "Oh my gosh! I love him."

"I know, right?"

"Wait till you see the ones I have." Lacy reached into her bag and pulled out three more magazines. She flipped to the center of one, where the same boy with floppy brown hair and puffy lips took up two whole pages of the magazine. Yuck. Taylor Daniels.

"He's even cuter with his shirt off." Sara giggled.

"I didn't know you were so crazy about Taylor Daniels." I watched Sara, wondering if she was just trying on a new personality like a new bathing suit.

"Of course!" Sara said.

"Isn't everyone? Well, almost everyone," Lacy said without looking at me, even though her words were totally meant for me. I knew this trick. Lacy probably thought it was so sly, but she wasn't the first snobby girl I'd come across in my life. She agreed with Sara in a way that made it obvious she totally disagreed with me.

The volleyball whizzed past my head and landed right on the picture of stupid Taylor Daniels. I bit my lip, secretly hoping Lacy would stand up and freak out at Tom and Derek, but she didn't. She spiked the ball back and ran over to join them.

It only took a few more minutes before other kids came around to play ball too. Kate and Emma waved at Sara and me. We smiled and waved back.

They were cold-water girls. I know for a fact because Emma and I took swimming lessons together last summer, and she never hogged the hot water.

"She came over after dinner yesterday," Sara said, like someone barging over after dinner meant you had to invite them to the pool, too. She twisted a chunk of her ponytail around her finger. "We're still on for Friday, right?"

Relieved that Sara was still Sara, I decided to ask her again if we could skim through her magazines for anything that might help with my mustache problem, but she said something just then that ruined everything.

"I invited Lacy too." Sara lifted her shoulders and raised her eyebrows, basically telling me I should be really excited she'd just invited hot-water Lacy to the special sleepover we'd been planning all summer—our last sleepover before sixth grade. The sleepover just after orientation where we were going to do makeovers and get rid of my mustache.

And maybe I didn't know it then, but it was the start of it all—how Lacy moved to Ohio from California just to ruin my life.

Chapter Five

Sara and I used to be able to sit in silence and be comfortable. The silence that stretched between us now stretched like a rubber band about to snap.

The sun sat high overhead, and even under the shade of the tree, sweat pooled behind my knees and in the crevices of my elbows. I really wanted to ask her why. Why did she ask Lacy to the sleepover? It had always been just us. We hadn't even invited Kate and Emma, even though we ate lunch with them at school. So, why the new girl? Why *this* girl?

I didn't know what bothered me more, Sara's silence or sitting so still. The heat aggravated my emotions and made me itch with even more questions. Was Sara still my best friend? And what was so great about Lacy and Taylor Daniels, or bikinis, for that matter?

"Let's play," I said, standing up.

"What? Volleyball? But you know I'm terrible. Please, Karma."

It struck me as funny in that not-really-funny way that Sara knew I knew things about her, like the fact that she hated sports, but she didn't mind ignoring things like the fact that I wouldn't want sparkly, pink Lacy at our sleepover. Having Lacy there would be like me inviting Kiran to join Sara and me to discuss our periods or how to pop a zit so it wouldn't leave a scar. I shouldn't have had to explain that to Sara. I wanted to hit something—so volleyball it was.

"Fine, suit yourself." I easily moved into the circle between Lacy and Kate and waited for the ball to come in my direction. It came toward me and I bumped the ball across the circle to Tom.

"Nice one, Karma," Derek said. He shook his hair out of his eyes and smiled at me, lifting his chin the way Kiran does when girls wave at him.

Lacy raised her eyebrows at me. I tried to shrug Derek's comment off, but I didn't know why Derek had said that with a smile, and I didn't know why it made my arms wobbly and numb in a nervous and self-conscious kind of way.

Lacy smirked and wouldn't stop glancing at me. She was the kind of girl with magnifying glasses for eyeballs. If she noticed my wobbly arms, she'd probably notice my mustache, too. I curled my lips into my mouth, fighting the urge to rub at the hair. I just hoped everyone had their eyes on the ball and wasn't paying attention to me.

Tom bumped the ball right between Lacy and me. I eyed Lacy. Her eyes were trained on the ball, but like a typical amateur, she wasn't in a hitting stance. The ball arched high enough, so I knew I could spike it back. I decided Lacy needed to know that I was Sara's friend and no way could she barge into my life and steal Sara away from me. So what if I didn't wear a bikini?

If I could get in front of her and smack the ball down with enough force, maybe she'd realize she'd picked the wrong house in the wrong town to move into. Her sparkles might have distracted Sara for the moment, but I'd show Sara that that was all Lacy was—a distraction.

I sidestepped, trying to get in front of Lacy. Just as I did, she finally braced to bump the ball, but it was too late. I was already right in front of her. I swung my arm. It would have been a perfect spike, but Lacy wouldn't give up. Her hand hit my elbow, knocking the ball off at an odd angle. Right at Sara.

For that split second before the ball hit her, Sara's face changed from surprised to confused at the sudden attention. Then the ball hit her nose with an ice-cream-onto-the-sidewalk kind of splat.

"Oh my gosh!" Lacy said, running toward Sara.

"Oh, man," Derek mumbled, shaking his head at me.

"Whoa. Isn't she your best friend?" Tom asked.

"It was an accident." I rushed over to Sara. "Are you okay? I'm so sorry."

Lacy pulled back from Sara and looked right at me. "Way to go, Karma. Her nose is bleeding."

Sara wouldn't lift her eyes. She held her nose and put her head down. Blood had dripped onto the top of her new two-piece bathing suit and dribbled onto her exposed stomach. Lacy held on to Sara's arm as she dug around for some tissues in her bag.

"Should we get a lifeguard?" Derek asked.

"No," Sara said. "I'm fine." Her voice was too loud and shaky. She wasn't fine. And I also knew from my first aid training that the dusty tissues from Lacy's bag weren't sterile. Plus bloodied tissues should be disposed of properly and not wadded up and thrown to the side the way Lacy dealt with them. I was obviously more qualified to be taking control of this situation.

I knelt down next to Sara. "Listen, Sara. Does your head hurt? Do you know where you are?"

"My nose is bleeding, not my brain," Sara mumbled through a second handful of tissues Lacy had shoved under her nose

The whistle that ended adult swim blew, officially ending our game and sending almost everyone back into the pool. Tom and Derek hovered nearby with the ball.

Lacy moved between Sara and me, blocking Sara's face from view. I fought the urge to snatch my things as she shoved my bag out of the way, flinging my sunscreen and books across the towels.

Lacy dabbed at Sara's nose. She used an ooey-gooey voice as she talked to Sara. Like anyone would really buy it that she knew Sara better than me.

I sat back and let Lacy think she'd won this time. But I knew something she didn't. Sara could never say no to an ice cream sandwich.

"Hey, I'll go buy us some ice cream sandwiches," I said, hoping the mention of an ice cream sandwich would make Sara forget I'd hit her in the face with a volleyball.

"Yeah," Lacy said. "The cold will probably help the bleeding stop." She grabbed Sara by the arm and helped her up.

I moved forward to walk on the other side of Sara, but Lacy somehow managed to get in my way. I considered saying a couple of *Satnam Wahegurus* just to calm myself down, but chose to take some deep breaths instead, mostly because Lacy didn't deserve anything heartfelt or sincere from me.

"I'll buy yours," Lacy said to Sara, butting into the conversation the same way she had butted into my life. "You need a free ice cream after all this." She turned enough to fake smile my way. Sara was too preoccupied with ignoring me to notice Lacy's sneer.

Tom and Derek came running from behind.

"Wait for us," Tom said, trying to leapfrog over Derek. They both ended up in another shoving match on the ground.

Lacy paid for Sara's ice cream and led her over to a table without even waiting for me. I paid for mine and hovered next to Sara. She scooted over but didn't bother to otherwise acknowledge me. I sat down, staring at my ice cream sandwich. I didn't really want it anymore. How could I eat something so sweet and cold when I felt so sour and hot inside?

"I dare you to eat that in one bite," Derek said to Tom, pointing at Tom's ice cream sandwich.

Tom shoved the whole thing into his mouth. White, melted ice cream leaked out of the sides of his mouth and dripped down to his chin.

"Ewww," Lacy squealed, throwing a napkin at him.

Tom jumped around, hitting himself in the head and hopping on one leg. He bumped into the picnic table, spilling Derek's can of Coke. It dribbled between the cracks, making Lacy and Sara yell and laugh.

"Gross, it's all over my legs!" Sara jumped up and threw a chunk of her ice cream sandwich at Tom.

I sat back, eyeing Mrs. Parker, who worked at the snack bar, hoping she wouldn't yell at us. Thankfully, she was busy turning hot dogs.

Sara dodged a piece of ice cream that Derek had thrown, and handed Lacy some napkins.

They both started to tear them and ball them up, before throwing napkin wads at the boys. I'd never glimpsed this side of Sara before. Sure, we'd goof off with Kate and Emma at lunch or during PE, but I'd never seen Sara so not-Sara in front of boys before. She had just joined in the silliness as though she'd always wanted to. It surprised me the same way her wearing the two-piece bathing suit, saying Derek was cute, and ogling over Taylor Daniels had. Maybe I'd been holding her back and Lacy was able to bring out Sara's silly side because Lacy was more fun and interesting than me.

Two ladies with small kids sitting at the next table shook their heads at us and dragged their kids back to the baby pool. I caught Mrs. Parker finally noticing us and scowling in our direction. She walked out from behind the counter.

"You guys need to clean all this up and keep it down," she said.

"We're really sorry," Tom said in his talking-to-adults voice. "Just a bad case of brain-freeze."

Sara giggled, which surprised me, because Mrs. Parker had been working at the pool and giving Sara and me ice cream sandwiches since we were in diapers. Trashing the snack area and laughing at Mrs.

Parker wasn't something Sara would normally do.

Mrs. Parker cleared her throat and raised an eyebrow at me—like it was my fault that Sara had imitated Lacy and acted so rude—before walking back into the snack bar.

Tom and Derek started making fart noises in step with random people walking by. Lacy threw away a couple of napkins and sat down across from me. I took a bite of my ice cream sandwich, but with Lacy right across the table, I wished I'd grabbed my book so I could cover the lower half of my face. Her blue eyes made my arm hair stand on end.

"Hey, Kar," she said. "I couldn't tell in the shade under the trees, but you have hair—everywhere."

The bite of ice cream sandwich in my mouth didn't quite know what to do. The cookie part stuck to the roof of my mouth as the ice cream part slowly trickled its way down my throat and into my chest, where it lodged right behind my heart.

Sara, Tom, and Derek were suddenly frozen.

"Look, it's no big deal," Lacy said with a dramatic sigh. "I have lemon juice in my bag. I never go anywhere without some. You shouldn't either. It's a natural bleach. I use it for my hair, but it'll even help with that stuff on your face." She leaned in closer to me and dabbed at my upper lip. "Like the fuzz here."

Fuzz? Even from the corner of my eye, I could see Sara's face turn a dark red and Tom's and Derek's shoulders shake.

Lacy slapped her hands down onto the table. "What?"

The rickety picnic table shook. I knew the laughing was making the table shake, but for a moment I hoped it was an earthquake—a big, ground-ripping earthquake that would open below me and swallow me whole.

"Dang, Karma!" Tom said, leaning in closer. "That's thicker than the 'stache I've been trying to grow all summer."

Derek punched him on the shoulder. "Man, stop it." But he laughed as Tom jumped onto the table and got close to my face. "'Stache Attack!" He put his index finger over his mouth in a finger mustache.

Lacy laughed, so Derek did the same and jumped in front of her. "You've been 'Stached!"

Lacy shoved Derek away. "Oh my gosh. Your breath smells like Coke."

I bet they wouldn't have even noticed my hair

if it hadn't been for Lacy and her big mouth. Sara would definitely see now that inviting Lacy here *and* to our sleepover was a huge mistake.

Sara didn't laugh, but she didn't say anything either. Angry red splotches formed up and down her neck. Or maybe they were annoyed red splotches. Or embarrassed red splotches—embarrassed of *me* red splotches. She sat there folding and unfolding her ice cream wrapper in long rectangles.

I wasn't asking for much, just for her to open her mouth and say, "It's not a mustache. Leave her alone." Was that too much to expect from my best friend? I remembered smelling *her* overalls in second grade in front of all the kids at recess, saying they didn't smell at all like pee, even though they did. I'd dried them under the hand dryer while she'd waited in the bathroom stall with nothing on but her underwear and shirt. Was wanting her to stand up for me right now asking for any more than a returned favor?

I guessed so, because Lacy dragged her off with Derek and Tom to jump into the deep end. When Tom yelled "'Stache Attack" and did a cannonball into the pool, Sara didn't even turn around and give me a smile or a shrug. Nothing. Nothing to reassure me it was just a joke and didn't mean anything.

I looked at the clock. Noon. Daddy was supposed to pick me up at three, but I didn't want to wait around, getting laughed at until then. I'd rather lie and tell him Sara dropped me off. I grabbed my bag and towel and left. If Sara noticed, she didn't come over to try to stop me. Even though I'd been in the shade most of the time and had lathered myself with SPF 45, every part of my body—inside and out—felt sunburned.

Not only had Lacy weaseled her way into the slumber party and our class, but she'd managed to wedge herself right between Sara and me the way an annoying piece of spinach gets stuck between your teeth. The more you fiddle with it, the slimier and more slippery it gets.

There was only one thing to do—stop her slimy hands from squirming further between Sara and me, stealing her away for good.

Chapter Six

Halfway up the stairs to my bedroom, Daddy caught me. My skin tingled with the sweaty stickiness of having been at the pool.

"Home so early, *beta*?"

"Yep. Sara's mom forgot she had a dentist appointment, so she dropped me off." I stood on the steps with my back to Daddy. It was silly, but sometimes I felt that other people could tell what had happened by just looking at my eyes. I couldn't turn around and let Daddy find out about 'Stache Attack or Lacy or the fact that Sara had morphed into a completely different person. I needed to go to my room and be alone. I couldn't sort through my embarrassment and confusion with someone watching.

"Cha leni?"

"No, thanks." Tea was Daddy's answer for everything. "I have a headache." Which I did. "And it's super hot outside." Which it was.

"Okay, *beta.*" Daddy hum-whistled tunelessly and headed back to his study, totally unaware how easily I'd lied to him.

Inside the bathroom I leaned over the sink and turned my head at different angles. The hairs were still there, like a pencil smudge above my mouth. No wonder Lacy had noticed it. Thanks to her turning it into a big joke with Tom and Derek, Sara had been too embarrassed to even stick up for me, much less help me figure out a way to get rid of it.

I needed a shower.

I let the hot water form tears on my face, because no real ones would come. Then I did what I'd started to do last summer when I needed to cry but couldn't. I thought about Dadima.

She died last year after living with us for two years. Even though Mom only worked part-time then, Dadima did most of the cooking. When she wasn't cooking, she'd teach me Punjabi. Daddy had taught me the alphabet and how to count, and he spoke Punjabi around the house, so that the sounds had been familiar enough for me to understand, even if I hadn't always known how to answer. But it didn't all fall into place until Dadima taught me to read.

She'd read me her prayer book and tell me stories about the gurus. She taught me things that I'd only read glimpses of on the projector screens at the gurdwara, when the Punjabi phrases from our Bible were projected with English translations under them as the priests sang. Sara went to Sunday school at her church, but the small and only gurdwara near Creekview didn't have anything like that. Dadima had been my Punjabi Sunday school.

I still smelled things that reminded me of her— the coppery smell of dirt and spices that had arrived with her from India the first day she came to live with us, the smell that went straight to the back of my nose and stuck to my throat. Daddy said it was the smell of India and his childhood. To me it was the smell of comfort.

I let the shower pour over me and wished it would make me shrink or disappear so I wouldn't have to face the world ever again. But the water got too cold, and I turned it off.

Wrapped in a towel, I leaned in close to the mirror so I could examine my face for the hundredth time. I needed to come up with a plan. Maybe I should give lemon juice a try, even though Lacy had suggested it. She might be my enemy, but I couldn't deny her style and sparkle, no matter how much I wanted to.

There were only four more days until school started. I just hoped 'Stache Attack wouldn't catch on before then.

Mom had been late or missed dinner completely all summer, since she'd started working full-time at the University of Creekview, the very university that hadn't renewed Daddy's research funding and was the reason he now stayed at home full-time. It also happened to be the same university that had promoted Mom from a summer-and-sometimes-night-class professor to co-head of the Department of Chemistry. It was some initiative to get more girls interested in studying science.

That night was no exception. Mom still hadn't returned home when Daddy put dinner on the table.

Kiran sat across from me. I watched him stab the fish on his plate with a fork instead of eat it.

He managed to get most of the curry off his fish and eat it plain. Daddy noticed and breathed hard out of his nose. I took a big bite, hoping if I ate and talked as if things were perfectly normal and not upside-down wrong, it would rub off on everyone else and we could pretend things were going smoothly.

"School starts Monday," I said, trying to start the conversation.

"Hmm," Daddy mumbled through a bite of rice and fish curry.

"Phht." Kiran made a sound through his teeth.

"So . . ." I stalled, rifling through my brain for a topic that wouldn't make Daddy and Kiran fight. Nothing came to mind.

The only sound any of us made was when our forks hit our plates, until Mom pushed through the garage door that opened into the kitchen.

"You're eating already?" she asked.

"It's seven o'clock," Daddy said, scratching his beard just in front of his ear, where it twisted into his turban.

"Oh." Mom put her bags down and pushed her dark blond hair off her forehead. "Well, I'm starved."

She smiled a smile that didn't reach her eyes—it

just kind of settled in her cheeks. Her entire body drooped the way an empty bag sags.

Daddy inhaled, about to say something.

I hopped up and grabbed a plate and fork for Mom before he could say anything that'd ruin Mom's mood more. Then I filled up a cup with ice water and set it at her spot.

"Thanks, love," she said as she scooped rice onto her plate. "How are things around here? Good?"

Daddy shrugged.

Kiran nodded.

"Yeah. Great," I said, doing my best to fill in all the empty, silent spaces. But really, instead of filling any gaps, my words bounced around the room, exposing each and every piece of awkwardness.

"Kiran," Mom said after she'd had a few bites, "Mrs. Moore called while I was in my meeting. Give her a call in the morning. She mentioned something about needing help in her garage."

"She *could* just call me," Kiran said. "Oh, wait. I don't have a phone."

"Kiran—" Mom started.

"Excuse me," Daddy said, breaking in. A piece of rice clung to his beard. "You work, so buy your own phone. We've already discussed this."

"This fish is really nice, Daddy. Is it fresh or frozen?" I asked, throwing my bouncy ball of conversation out as a distraction.

"Whatever." Kiran stood up to leave the table.

"We're still eating, young man," Daddy said in a voice that he clearly tried to keep steady.

"Fine." Kiran sat back down but didn't touch his plate.

"Raj," Mom said, reaching across the table for Daddy's hand.

Daddy pulled his hand back and shoveled another bite into his mouth. "The school sent over your finalized schedule."

Kiran squirmed in his chair, suddenly intensely interested in the fish curry on his plate.

"I don't remember authorizing two periods of band. What happened to advanced biology?" Daddy tapped his fork on the edge of his plate.

Tink. Tink. Tink.

"Do you know that frozen fish is actually more fresh—" I began.

Mom cleared her throat and raised her eyebrows at me. She then turned to Daddy. "Do we need to discuss this now? I just got home, we're eating . . ."

"Did you know something about this, Mary?"

54

Daddy asked, rubbing his beard the same way he did when Mom mentioned the university. The piece of rice that stuck to his beard fell onto the table.

"Well, actually." Mom chewed the fish slowly and wiped her mouth with a napkin. "Kiran is very talented, and his band teacher has given him the extra slot—"

"He's talented in the sciences, too. Will music pay the bills? No!" Daddy rose from his chair, his voice not so steady anymore. "Being a doctor, that's what will pay the bills. You don't push him. Instead you let him choose."

"You didn't let me explain," Mom said.

"I can explain for myself. I'm fourteen!" Kiran surprised us all with his outburst. We sat in a horror-movie silence as he shoved away from the table. "It's my life. I can make my own decisions. Anyway, how's that PhD working out for you?" Kiran's eyes shot to Daddy as he said the last comment and let it settle like chopped cilantro on a finished curry.

All I wanted was to add a cooling helping of yogurt to smooth everything over, but I was running out of things to say. Even if I'd wanted to talk about my crummy day, which I wasn't sure I did, Kiran's outburst stirred up enough tension that I released my worries about my mustache, Sara, Lacy, and 'Stache Attacks, letting them fly across the room like a balloon you blow up and let go. For now.

Instead I focused on my plate and listened to Kiran stomp up the stairs and slam his bedroom door shut. The repetitive riffs of his electric guitar were muffled through the floorboards.

Mom poked at her plate with her fork without taking a bite. Daddy pushed away from the table, left the room, and slammed the door to his study.

"I'll wash the dishes," I said with a smile that tried to slide across my mouth, the muscles in my face fighting back in confusion. It felt as if someone had stuck a smile sticker on my mouth. The same as Mom's after-work smile.

Chapter Seven

Eager to drown out the quiet that wound through the house like a giant python, I practiced my piano without having to be asked. I even went longer than the thirty minutes I typically trudged through. Then I grabbed all the recycling and went outside to divide it into the containers. This was actually Kiran's job, but I didn't bother making a big deal out of it. Not only because it'd set Daddy off again, but I wanted an excuse to get outside. All the air had been sucked out of the house after dinner, making it hard to breathe.

My head burst with questions, and not the easy-to-answer kind. That's why I liked math. There were formulas for everything. Want to know how much space is inside that triangle? Easy. A=1/2 bh.

No matter what shape or size the triangle, the formula's the same. Things in life should work out as easily. Follow a basic set of rules you've memorized, and it'll all work out.

I flipped through the stack of papers Daddy had put outside his study, distracting myself from trying to squish my problems into a formula. Most of the papers were printouts of how to create a website and write codes. Computer programming filled most of Daddy's nonworking hours these days. Pamphlets he'd grabbed at the temple a few weeks ago were buried inside the stack too. We didn't go often, only on the anniversary of Dadima's death and for Vaisakhi or Diwali. Yet whenever Daddy went to the temple, he grabbed stacks of pamphlets and he'd tell us in the car on the way home that we should go more often. But in the same way the pamphlets got stacked and restacked and finally put out in the recycling, so did Daddy's plans of going to the temple again.

A smaller paper fluttered out of the stack and landed on the porch. I balanced the papers on my knee and bent to pick the insert up from the floor. It read:

"Your Karma, Your Life"
A talk by Dr. Gurwinder Singh.
Come on the 23rd of September at 7 p.m.
for an enlightening discussion about
karma through the scriptures of Gurbani.

I tucked the paper into my back pocket. I used to love my name, but then I realized I could never find any pens or stickers with my name on them. Last year when Sara went on vacation, she found a bumper sticker that read *Keep Calm and Hug Karma*. I'd stuck it in the desk mirror in my bedroom. Now I collected anything with the word "karma" on it. I read the pamphlet again. *Your Karma, Your Life*. Actually, karma was kind of a formula. I mean, when you do good, good happens. It wasn't exactly as easy as that, but that's basically what it meant.

I'd asked Dadima a million questions about it, like what if I stepped on an ant on the sidewalk but didn't mean to or didn't even know I'd done it, would I still be punished? Dadima explained that it had more to do with my heart, and she told me to pray and recite *Naam*, like saying *Satnam Waheguru*.

I'd rather be safe and say my *Satnam*s than end

up a squished ant in my next life. But that had also been something I'd worried about. How could I be blamed for my past if I didn't even remember it? Dadima had told me to stop worrying about it, but I never could. If Daddy was in a better mood later, maybe I'd ask him about going to the talk.

After I dragged all the recycling out to the road, the phone's loud trill cut through the quiet night air. I wanted it to be Sara, and I also didn't want it to be Sara. It wasn't just today at the pool, but the bra and Oreo incident mixed with her silence today, making me question my friendship with her. She hadn't wanted to talk-talk so much anymore even before she'd gone away on vacation. It was almost like she wished she were somewhere else instead of hanging out with me.

I just knew something had shifted in a way that made me unsure how to act around her or what exactly the state of our friendship was. Of course we'd both changed. Our feet had grown a complete shoe size since last year, and Sara had grown her bangs out, but it was more than that. It was like how wearing blue or pink goggles in the pool changes the color of everything. I kept wearing my same clear goggles, and Sara chose to wear green ones. We were in all the same places but were seeing things so differently.

"Karmajeet," Daddy called.

I walked back inside toward the kitchen. Daddy stood outside his study with the phone in his hand.

"For you," he said, handing me the phone. "Five minutes."

That was what he always said. But because the questions and confusion I'd carried around all day were finally catching up with me, making me feel sore, I said, *"Hanji."*

"Hello?" I said into the phone.

"Hi, Karma."

My cheeks flushed at Sara's voice, and a small ringing clanged in my ears as I pictured her sitting at the snack bar, folding her ice cream sandwich wrapper and not telling Lacy to disappear when she announced my mustache to the world.

I managed a "Hi."

"Listen, I'm sorry about this afternoon. I didn't know you left. I thought you just went to the bathroom."

"Oh."

"Really. I promise," Sara said, her voice so serious, I almost believed her. Then I remembered that

I'd smashed her nose with the volleyball. If karma was a formula, then me smashing the volleyball in Sara's face meant I kind of deserved for Lacy to make fun of me.

"How's your nose?"

"Fine. It doesn't even hurt."

"I'm sorry. It really was an accident."

"I know. And you know, Lacy was just trying to help. That's all."

"Help? Tom and Derek made fun of me."

"Well, she didn't mean it like that. And since when do you care what Tom and Derek think anyway?"

"I don't. I guess." Did I?

"Look, I'll find that article in *Teen Bop* about facial hair. I'll even pull out my issues from last year too. I kind of forgot about it, plus I didn't think you'd want me to show it to you with everyone else around," Sara said.

I bit my lip. "Facial hair" sounded so extreme. But I had asked Sara what to do, and even if I didn't believe that Lacy had really been trying to help, Sara wouldn't deliberately hurt me. She might be distracted and acting different, but under all of that she was still my Sara.

"We'll scour the magazines after orientation.

Don't worry. I'm sure no one is going to notice it. I mean, come on, the boys were just being stupid. They were totally exaggerating. I think everyone's going to be too busy noticing Derek's blackheads and the fact that Tom's nose has, like, doubled in size since last year."

Sara was being goofy and trying to make me feel better, but I just couldn't 100 percent believe that no one else would notice my mustache or make fun of it. "I don't know—"

"Ugh, Karma. I'm serious," Sara said with a sigh. "Not everything is totally about you, okay? Look, no one even brought it up again after you left. Seriously. My mom took Lacy and me to get snacks and nail polish this afternoon. You really should have hung around."

"It was really hot, and I had a headache." It was a lame excuse when I'd said it to Daddy, and it sounded even more pathetic trying it on Sara.

"I've been writing out the sleepover schedule," Sara said, skimming over my excuse. "We'll start out with facials because our pores need lots of time to steam open before we apply masks before bed. Lacy has this completely natural recipe she said we can whip up in the blender."

Just the mention of Lacy made my chest tingle the way it did after eating chicken curry when Daddy makes it too spicy. But Sara and I had been planning our back-to-school sleepover all summer, and I wasn't going to let Lacy ruin it.

"I can't wait." I tried to say it with more excitement than I felt.

"Really?" Sara asked. "Good. Plus my mom said she'll take us out to Supremo's for dinner right after orientation."

"Even better," I said. "Do you remember the last time we went there?"

Sara genuinely laughed for the first time in a long time. "Are you serious? How could I forget? I don't even remember what was so funny, but I still remember the burn from snorting Coke out my nose." I smiled to myself, letting our shared memory erase some of the strangeness that hung between us.

Keep Calm and Hug Karma. I let those words settle around me. I must have been overreacting about this whole Lacy thing. Tom and Derek had teased me and started the stupid 'Stache Attack joke because they'd been showing off for Lacy. It totally wouldn't catch on.

Plus, Sara and Lacy weren't the only ones who could plan makeovers.

Once I'd hung up with Sara, I went upstairs and locked myself in the bathroom. I knew Mom kept her makeup on the top shelf of the medicine cabinet. I grabbed a bottle of foundation and closed the cabinet.

The label said to use my ring fingers to massage it into my face. I squirted a dime-size dot onto my hand like I'd seen Mom do a million times before. Then I dipped my right ring finger in and dotted the foundation around my face, mostly paying attention to my mustache area.

Once I'd rubbed it all in, I stared at my face from every angle. I liked how it made my skin feel soft, but it didn't cover up my mustache all that much. I did look different, though. Older. I opened the cabinet and grabbed Mom's brown eyeliner. Sara had already showed me an article this summer about how to use it on your upper lid to make your eyes *pop*. Maybe if I could make my eyes pop, no one would even notice my mustache.

It was harder to do than it looked in the magazine, but I managed to get my left eye better than my right. I stood back to take in the whole look.

It looked all right. I wouldn't be able to pull it off every day because Mom would notice her foundation emptying too fast, and Daddy would go into lecture mode, "The Shabad says when you adorn yourself with paint, you are giving up control of your body and conforming to the world's standards. Be glad Babaji created you so perfectly."

Eye roll. Yeah, so perfect that I now had a nickname. Plus, I'm pretty sure every lady in his beloved Bollywood films wore several layers of makeup, along with jewelry and false eyelashes. I might be willing to bend the rules a bit with makeup or even lemon juice like Lacy suggested, but Daddy would really lose it if I did something drastic, like waxing. Mom's blond hair didn't grow where it wasn't supposed to. It's not like she had stuff like wax strips and tweezers just lying around. I'd have to keep it simple and hopefully come up with a more permanent plan before school actually started.

Chapter Eight

addy whistled loudly and shrilly as we walked down the street toward school for orientation. If Bollywood music on the radio sounded like a bird being strangled, then Daddy's whistling without the help of the radio sounded like a bird with a seed stuck in its throat.

Our street snaked around a bend that led down to the school. My throat tightened and the insides of my ears tingled as I looked at Holly Creek Middle School. It was a huge, three-story building with lots of places to get turned around in and lost.

My old elementary school sat across the intersection from the middle school. The several one-story buildings scattered about, separated by playgrounds and gardens, suddenly looked small and babyish in comparison.

In the bathroom at home Mom's makeup had looked good, and then when I'd put on the pink shirt with the puckered sleeves, I'd felt older and ready. But the quick glances I caught of myself in the windows of the cars parked along the street showed the regular old me.

I shrugged my sleepover bag further up my shoulder and wished I'd changed my shirt like I'd wanted to before I left. Daddy had rushed me out the door before I could change, eager to get to school and meet my teachers.

I wasn't ready for this. Maybe I had a fever. I definitely felt sweaty and light-headed. When I swallowed, my throat felt scratchy. Maybe I had strep throat.

The fact that Sara would be with me at orientation and that I'd be going to her house afterward for a sleepover were the only things keeping me from freaking out about anyone noticing my mustache. Having Sara at my side still made the big things seem less big.

I jogged ahead a few steps to catch up to Daddy.

"Learning is so exciting, *beta*," Daddy said. "You should be running, not shuffling behind me."

"Hanji." Daddy didn't worry about clothes or friends or mustaches when he thought about school. All he worried about were classes and teachers.

We walked through the side gate and followed the sidewalk around the packed parking lot. Sara stood at the front of the school, leaning against a pillar near the entrance to the auditorium.

"Sara," I called, and ran toward her.

"My mom left me her keys. She went in to meet the teachers. Let's take your bag to my car."

Daddy reached us and said hi to Sara. "I'll meet you inside," he said to me.

We tossed my bag into the backseat of Sara's car and turned to go inside the school. Sara stopped between the cars and pulled at her skirt and fluffed her hair at the scalp. If only hair volume was the worst of my problems.

"I thought you were going to wear that skirt on the first day of school," I said.

"Oh, well, last night Lacy said I should wear it today. I'm borrowing one of hers for the first day."

I cleared my throat, trying to get rid of the uncomfortable burn that surged through my body at the mention of Lacy and Sara talking last night.

69

When Sara had called me, it'd ended on a note like things were how they used to be—easy and comfortable. But knowing she'd also talked to Lacy turned all of that inside out, which made me shaky and confused. I didn't know if I was mad or jealous or hurt or just tired.

The mention of Lacy's name made me want to lash out at Sara, not to hurt her, just defend myself.

"My mom let me borrow her makeup." I leaned closer to the car window and turned my head side to side like I could really see the difference the makeup had made.

"You're lucky. I'm only allowed to wear tinted lip gloss, and"—she paused, putting her hand on her hip and pointing a finger at me to imitate her mom—"that's it."

I cracked up because Sara mimicked voices really well. She used to do voice impressions all the time to make Ruthie stop crying.

Sara gave a final tug to the sides of her skirt and sighed. "I can't believe we're starting middle school."

"You've been talking about it *all* summer," I said. I wanted to laugh, but then I saw Sara's face.

All summer she'd shrugged off all my crazy

freak-outs, but now, fidgeting with her skirt, she looked like the Sara I'd met in kindergarten. Shy, quiet, and crying in a corner. She'd done that for a whole week. Then she'd spilled her juice and I'd shared my animal crackers with her. We'd been best friends ever since.

Sara let out a long sigh. "I know." We looped arms and scurried toward the school. "That shirt is perfect, by the way. I'm glad you wore it."

When we reached the pillars in front of school, Sara stopped. "Listen, Karma. Let's meet here Monday. Right here at this pillar. The buses stop all along here, but we'll meet at this pillar before school, and then we won't have to walk inside alone."

"Perfect!" My head still hurt, but my shoulders relaxed slightly, now that I knew I wouldn't walk into school alone on the first day. As we pushed through the doors into the building, the noise and size of the place seemed too big. Even with all the kids and parents inside, there were large gaps of empty space.

Having Sara next to me shrunk my worries about Lacy, my mustache, and everything middle school small enough that I could almost pretend they didn't exist.

It wasn't until our parents came with us to meet our teacher in homeroom that I could completely forget about Lacy, Tom, Derek, and 'Stache Attack. I was so afraid Daddy would ask a million questions that I couldn't pay attention to anything else.

And, of course, Daddy asked the first question. "Will you provide the students with a list of supplementary activities and lessons?" Ms. Hillary, the oldest teacher ever, got excited and discussed the new after-school groups that were starting this year to extend our learning outside the classroom. Thankfully Derek's dad followed Daddy's question with one about dress code and haircuts that made Derek's neck turn red.

After orientation my head throbbed and hurt too much for me to pretend I didn't care that Lacy was riding with us. I tried to smile the entire ten-minute ride to Sara's house, but I knew I'd have fake-smile eyes, the kind that scrunch up like the crusty edges of burned toast. And then when Lacy ran across the street to her house to pick up her stuff, I did my best to blink away the idea that Lacy didn't even really have to pack a bag. She lived across the street. The street that divided our middle school from our old elementary school had seemed like an ocean too big to swim across, but the street between Sara's and Lacy's houses was more like a bridge connecting them.

"Let me get Ruthie ready, and we'll be off to dinner in about an hour, girls," Mrs. Green called as we ran upstairs to Sara's room.

I threw my bag to the side of Sara's bed and fell back onto her yellow-and-white comforter. She had decorated her room in the fourth grade when we were obsessed with sunflowers, and her room hadn't changed much since. She had stuck more things onto the boards that hung on her walls. The photos of us together over the past couple of years were still there, but she'd added some new cutouts from magazines and a photo of her and her cousin at the beach. She'd gotten the idea for the boards from a magazine about redecorating your room with things you already had lying around your house. That was back when we were still reading *Highlights* and *American Girl* magazines.

I pushed myself up onto my elbows and realized that unless we slept in the basement, one of us would have to sleep on the floor. Usually Sara and I squished into her bed, but with Lacy spending the night too, someone would end up sleeping alone. My stomach did a flip.

I repeated *Satnam Waheguru,* telling my fears to disappear, at least for now so I could enjoy this sleepover with my best friend, even if it meant spending time with Lacy and giving up my space on the bed.

Ruthie burst into Sara's room and jumped onto my lap.

"Hey, you," I said, hugging her back.

"Mom said you can paint my fingernails." Ruthie bounced down and grabbed the bottle of purple polish off Sara's dresser. There were about four colors lined up, with a little silver dish holding cotton balls next to a bottle of polish remover.

"Ruthie, don't mess it up," Sara said.

"Mom said I can." Ruthie put both her hands around the polish and stuck her tongue out at Sara.

"I'll do it," I said. "Here, Ruthie. Give me the bottle and we'll paint your nails."

Ruthie squealed and handed me the bottle. Sara went over to the dresser to straighten up the polish.

Ruthie's nails were so tiny, it only took me one coat of polish and a couple of minutes to finish.

Lacy came through Sara's door as I gave Ruthie's nails a final dab.

"Lacy, Lacy, Lacy!" Ruthie jumped up and knocked the polish over with her knee before I had the chance to screw the cap on all the way. A small drip of purple nail polish puddled on Sara's carpet.

"Ruthie!" Sara yelled. "Quick, Karma, grab the remover."

Most of it came up when I rubbed at it for a minute, but I had to turn my face at the smell of the polish remover because it made my head throb.

"It got all messy," Ruthie said, pouting at her fingernails.

Lacy took Ruthie's hand. "I can fix that, easy." She grabbed the clear polish off Sara's dresser and dabbed it onto Ruthie's nails. "See? Good as new. You should always use a topcoat. I learned that in surfing club."

"You *surf*?" Sara asked in a whispered voice that sent a prickle of weirdness to my cheeks.

"Sure."

"Have you ever seen a shark?" Ruthie asked, pushing herself between me, Sara, and Lacy.

"Go away, Ruthie, or I'm telling Mom you

spilled nail polish on the rug," Sara said, elbowing her away.

"Did you bring your surfboard with you?" Ruthie asked, elbowing Sara back.

"No, silly," Lacy said.

Ruthie giggled and squirmed past Sara and tripped over my knees to sit on Lacy's lap.

Seeing Ruthie on Lacy's lap made me want to stand up and tell Lacy she couldn't have Sara. And definitely not her family, too.

Ruthie turned toward me. "Can *you* surf?"

I shook my head. "No." It sounded so lame, so I added, "I play the piano, though."

"Yeah, I know. You and Sara both play." Ruthie jumped up. "I'm going to tell Mom that Lacy can surf!"

Lacy stood up and walked toward the photos Sara had pinned up near her closet. "Oh my gosh! Is this you, Karma?" Lacy asked, unsticking a photo of Sara and me.

The color had faded slightly, but you could see the original color on the corner where the picture had been covered by another photo since third grade. My sweater was a mix of pea green and mustard yellow, and my hair stuck out in all directions in a frizzy mess. We'd been to the fall festival in town, and both our hair had gotten staticky in the bouncy house. Of course right after, Sara's hair had fallen back into place, but mine had stayed puffy and crazy.

"That's hilarious!" Sara said. "I forgot about that sweater. You used to wear it all the time."

"Not *all* the time," I said, defensive about the sweater Dadima had knitted for me.

"It's so weird, because you still look *exactly* the same," Lacy said.

"You're right," Sara said. "You haven't changed at all since third grade, Kar."

I bit the inside of my cheek. I'd *definitely* changed. I didn't wear that sweater anymore. I'd gotten taller. . . .

Who was I kidding? My mustache was the only noticeable change. Obviously, facial hair wasn't the kind of change Sara and Lacy were talking about. I didn't want them to be right. I especially didn't want Lacy to *know* she was right. There had to be something I could say, but before anything came to mind, Lacy turned to Sara.

"You were so adorable!" Lacy said. "But your hair definitely suits you much better now. You know, all long with layers. It frames your cheekbones so well."

Sara sat up straighter on her bed and smiled.

I'd only been at Sara's for twenty minutes, and already Lacy had managed to flatter Sara, win over Ruthie, and make me question everything about myself even more than normal. I didn't even think that was possible.

Earlier I might have been worried about strep throat or my mustache being a sign of an unknown disease, but now what freaked me out was the idea that instead of me being able to solve a single problem, Lacy would just keep finding more and more things I needed to fix about myself.

Sara's mom poked her head into the room and told us we had to be downstairs in thirty minutes. There were only a handful of places to go out to dinner in our town, and Supremo's was by far our favorite. Most of the other families probably had the same idea.

Lacy dug through her bag and pulled out a small pouch. "All right. Who's up for a makeover?"

"I can't," Sara said. "I'm only allowed lip gloss."

"I can do that." Lacy grabbed a tube and dabbed it on Sara. The smell of vanilla and strawberry filled the room, making me rub my neck.

"Here, Kar. I've got this mascara that would really make your eyes crazy pretty."

Before I could explain that Daddy would start quoting from the Shabad or that I'd already put on some makeup, she pulled me next to her and brushed at my eyelashes. It felt strange to have someone so close to my face and touching near my eyes. I sucked in my breath and waited for her to say something about my mustache, but she didn't.

"There. Take a look." She stood next to me, staring back at me in the mirror.

I blinked a couple of times, trying to get used to the sticky feeling. My eyes did look bigger and more open.

"You can have this if you want. It'll definitely make people focus on your eyes instead of the hair here." Lacy tapped the top of her mouth.

Just when I'd thought I might be able to actually like Lacy, she had to bring up my mustache. I looked in the mirror at Sara's reflection. She had her eyes focused on her fingernails, like the bright pink she'd chosen was the most interesting thing in the world—more interesting than stopping Lacy from making fun of my mustache. *Again.*

If I didn't figure out before Monday how to get rid of my mustache permanently and prove to Sara that Lacy wasn't really the friend Sara thought she was, I'd be walking the halls of Holly Creek Middle School all by myself.

Chapter Nine

We all squeezed into the back of Sara's van because Ruthie wanted both Lacy and me to sit next to her. Sara didn't want to be in front and have to turn around to talk to us, so she squished next to me, closer to the window. Ruthie's car seat dug into my hip, but I ignored the pain because sitting like this, no matter how uncomfortable, was the closest I'd been to Sara the entire afternoon.

Now that I finally had her so close, I didn't know what to say. When I scratched my knee, the dark purple nail polish I'd decided on after Lacy had insisted on painting my nails made me think someone else's hands were touching my leg.

My stomach did a funny rumble thing, and the

fake-fruit smell of Lacy's lip gloss didn't help.

Ruthie started to sing a song about spaghetti and meatballs, and when I scrunched my face to smile at her, it made my head ache again.

We pulled into Supremo's parking lot, and Sara grabbed a brush from her purse and started to fret over her split ends.

"Don't worry. No one will notice them. Just use that avocado-and-banana hair mask Sunday night. Your hair will be so shiny. Trust me," Lacy said, handing Sara her lip gloss.

"Avocado and banana?" I asked, willing my stomach to hold steady. I didn't know if the combination of the avocado and banana had caused my stomach to cramp, or the fact that Lacy and Sara had talked about so many things without me around. I knew they'd shopped for the nail polish and talked on the phone, but how much did they talk about without me?

"Yeah," Sara said. "We read an article about it in *Teen Bop*. It's supposed to work better than the mayonnaise we did last time."

I had to swallow. Sara and I had put half a jar of mayonnaise in our hair at the beginning of summer to smooth out the frizz. The only thing it did was make us smell like egg salad for the entire day, even after we used her coconut shampoo four times to wash it out.

Remembering that vinegary smell made the car feel way too hot and squished. I sucked in a huge gulp of fresh night air the minute Mrs. Green found a parking place and we piled out of the van.

The doors of Supremo's opened with a swoosh that sucked us into the packed waiting area. We stood back as Mrs. Green put her name on the waiting list. She was right, lots of other families had had the same idea. There were kids I recognized from elementary school but lots of kids I didn't recognize at all.

Lacy and Sara giggled together as we waited. I reached for Ruthie's hand, but she already had hold of her mom's.

Lacy smiled and waved at a few older girls and even a few of the boys. I didn't know how she could possibly know any of them just from a couple of hours at orientation and one trip to the pool. Sure, we lived in a small town, but she'd been here less than a week.

Sara and Lacy traded shoes while we waited. They both wore slip-on shoes that had cute little cutouts at their toes, which showed their bright pink toenails. I'd chosen the dark purple for my toes and fingers, but they'd chosen to go pink on their toes and light purple on their fingers.

Something about seeing their matching shoes and nail polish sent a surge of panic through me. Did everyone know something I didn't? But worse, no one—not even Sara—wanted to tell me?

Dread squirreled its way down my chest, mixing with my sense of aloneness, making my stomach do a funny gurgle, but not because I was hungry.

It must have showed on my face, because as we scooted into the curved booth several minutes later, Mrs. Green asked, "You okay, Karma?"

"You do look a little funny," Sara said. "Are you all right?"

I tried to smile because I already felt like an annoying, wobbly wheel on a grocery cart and didn't want to give Sara more reasons to choose Lacy over me.

Mrs. Green asked what we wanted on our pizza. I nodded and shrugged at all the suggestions, even Lacy's about a California Special.

Our half-circle booth sat near the back of the restaurant. I couldn't help but feel on display, even though I knew everyone was too busy staring at brand-new Lacy, not me. A lot of boys walked past our booth on their way to the bathroom, even though they could have just walked the other way around the circle table in front of us.

The pizza came covered in a mixture of green, squishy stuff and shriveled red things. I put my hand over my mouth and swallowed.

"You guys are going to love this!" Lacy clapped. "It's avocado and sundried tomatoes."

That was all it took. The mushy contents of my stomach splattered all over the floor in full view of everyone in Supremo's. And unlike all those gawking boys, I didn't make it to the bathroom.

Chapter Ten

My life in sixth grade had come to an end before it had even begun.

I lay on my bed, staring at the ceiling. It mocked me with its boring ordinariness. Its stark white paint and smooth surface stretched throughout my room and house and probably every house in the country.

A ceiling. A typical, plain ceiling. Why couldn't *my life* be typical and plain?

After I'd thrown up, Mrs. Green had asked for the pizza to be boxed up, and she'd driven me home, letting me sit in the front seat. I'd been too upset to even worry about whether I was breaking a federal law and car safety regulations by sitting in the front seat.

Sara walked me to the door, but when Mom opened it, I pretended to need the bathroom. I hadn't wanted to relive my humiliation by explaining to her what had happened. Mom had too much to worry about with work. I didn't want to add more problems, especially with Kiran acting so weird. So I brushed my teeth and buried myself in my bed.

Hours later I was still there, sifting through the confusion flooding my brain. The leftover embarrassment from last night tingled my face and arms. I wished I could box it up with the leftover pizza and stomp on it. Now instead of just being 'Stache Attack, I could be teased for throwing up too. Lacy would probably even come up with some kind of stupid nickname that included both, like Supremo 'Stache or El Hairy Puko. What if she and Sara had already come up with something last night?

When my stomach growled for the millionth time, I gave up trying to stay in bed all day and went downstairs.

There were no spicy smells to greet me in the kitchen, just the clattering of computer keys from Daddy's office.

"Morning, sweetie," Mom said.

I'd almost forgotten it was Saturday. Somehow

the simple fact that Mom was home made my life feel normal. "Morning, Mom."

I squeezed next to her for a sideways hug.

"You feeling better this morning?" she asked, pushing the back of her hand against my forehead. "You don't have a fever. Are you hungry? How about some toast?"

"Okay," I said, sliding onto a stool.

"I made a list of school supplies." Mom pushed a list across the counter to me.

Daddy had added a scientific calculator to Mom's list. Then I noticed the asterisk at the bottom of the page—*ask a saleslady about a training bra.*

Training bra?

"Mom, are you serious?"

"Well, it's time to think about these things."

Words started to form in my head to tell her about 'Stache Attack and ask what to do about my mustache. I opened my mouth, hoping Daddy would keep typing so he wouldn't be able to hear our conversation.

"What about—"

Mom's phone buzzed and rattled on the counter near the coffeepot just as I'd gotten the nerve to say what was in my head.

"Just a minute." She put the plate of toast in front of me and patted my hand before she grabbed her phone. "Dr. Khullar," she said instead of hello.

Daddy came out of his study with an empty teacup. "Morning, *beta*. All better?"

I nodded because Mom made huge gestures with her hand in our direction for us to be quiet.

Daddy being in the room squished the few words I'd managed to think of to bring up my mustache to Mom. Besides, the memory of Ruthie pointing out my mustache the afternoon of the Oreo incident and the barf fest at Supremo's still rubbed at me like a new pair of shoes, making me unsure if I really wanted to talk about it at all. Mom hadn't noticed the hair on my face. Why didn't she notice it, if Ruthie and Lacy had? Maybe Mom didn't pay attention to me as closely as everyone else anymore.

"Okay, fine. I'll be over in half an hour." Mom dropped her phone onto the counter. "Well, there goes my Saturday. You can take Karma shopping, can't you, Raj?"

But she wasn't really asking. She was already halfway up the stairs to get ready.

I shoved a piece of toast into my mouth because I didn't know what to say. I didn't even know how

I felt. Mom had always taken me school shopping. Sure, Daddy could take over the cooking, cleaning, and driving us around, but shopping for a bra?

Now not only would I not get a chance to talk to Mom about my mustache until she was back home and I got up the nerve again, but I'd have to buy a bra with Daddy. Meanwhile Lacy and Sara were probably still hanging out, having fun without me.

Chapter Eleven

I slept in my bra Sunday night. I wanted to be used to it before I had to actually wear it out in public, but when I got up Monday morning, it didn't feel any more normal than it had felt on Sunday. Mom said I was "developing" and should wear it even though I couldn't see the point. I mean, sure I'd noticed the bumps, but my T-shirts hid them okay. Not only had it been embarrassing to buy the bra, with Daddy pretending not to know me as the saleslady helped, but he wouldn't even say the word "bra" to the saleslady. He'd just kind of pointed in the general direction of underwear and asked the saleslady to help me. I usually put my new clothes into the laundry once I'd cut off the tags, but I couldn't imagine Daddy finding my bra in the washing.

I quickly escaped out of it and shoved it into my sock drawer before getting ready for school. I'd already picked out my clothes the night before, a purple T-shirt I already owned and the skirt with embroidery that I'd gotten from Sara. I even took an extra few minutes to smooth down my frizz halo. I pulled part of my hair back and kept it low, with a small piece falling just across my forehead. Lacy had worn her hair that way when we'd gone out to the dinner-I-never-wanted-to-talk-about-again.

After brushing my teeth, I spritzed some lemon juice I'd found at the back of the fridge onto my face and patted at my upper lip, evening out the lemon juice and trying to get it to soak in faster. I'd used it yesterday too, but I couldn't tell if it'd helped. I was willing to give anything a try at this point even if it had been Lacy's idea. Finally, I added a bit of eyeliner and brushed the mascara through my lashes a couple of times. I decided not to bother with the foundation, since it seemed to mostly rub off in a few hours anyway.

In the kitchen Mom stuffed her bag with binders and papers, and Daddy whistled at the stove, adding last-minute sprinkles of cilantro and salt to the dal.

"Morning," I said, trying to sound happier than I felt. Sara and I hadn't talked since my puke fest at Supremo's. I'd almost dialed her number a few times, but I'd been kind of waiting for her to call first. The weird silence between us made me incomplete, a puzzle with a missing piece—a big glaring hole of a piece that left the rest of the picture looking pointless and stupid.

Mom came toward me and gave me a hug. "You excited?"

I shrugged, trying to cut her hug short. I still hadn't forgiven her for making me shop for my first bra with Daddy.

"You smell nice. What is that?" Mom asked. "It's very citrusy."

I grabbed a bagel and shoved it into the toaster. I wanted to stuff all my annoyance with Mom, confusion with Sara, and frustration with myself into the toaster and burn it all up, but emotions didn't come in a convenient bagel shape, so I was left to shove them further into myself.

Kiran stumbled into the kitchen, rubbing his eyes. I think he only ever gave himself five minutes to eat and get ready in the morning. He held the fridge door open with his leg and pinched the back of my arm as I reached around him for the cream cheese.

I elbowed him in the shoulder.

Mom tried to straighten the collar of his shirt, but he ducked and grabbed half my bagel and his bag. "See ya."

I didn't bother arguing with him to give it back, because with the way I felt, I wasn't even sure I'd be able to keep down the other half of the bagel. With a sigh Mom turned back to me. "Well, here are a few things from the university. Even an extra eraser and folder for Sara. I know how much you girls like to match."

"Thanks," I said, even though I was pretty sure Sara's *Teen Bop* magazine had an entire back-to-school article on matching school supplies being so third grade.

Daddy picked the receipt for the folders up off the counter. "Not even a staff discount?"

"Oh, stop." Mom waved her hand, fanning his comment like a bad smell. "You know there's been budget cuts in every department."

"Yes. Yes, I do know about the budget cuts," Daddy said, tugging on his beard.

"That's not what I meant. I wasn't trying to

bring up what happened with the funding for your department." Mom sighed. "I've gotta go before traffic gets bad. Be back for dinner!" she called to no one and everyone.

Daddy cleared his throat a few times but didn't say anything else. I shoved the new school supplies into my bag, along with the stainless steel tiffin Daddy had packed. It had one compartment for dal and one for chapatis. The two pieces were flat bowls that stacked on top of each other and clicked together with a handle.

It was the same tiffin Dadima had used to pack for Daddy when she lived with us. Now that he didn't use it, he packed it for me. Since kindergarten Mom had packed my lunch box with sandwiches and wraps, but I liked that Daddy wanted to pack me a tiffin with rice and curries. The tiffin somehow made it feel like Dadima would be with me all day.

My fingers lingered on the handle, and I imagined Dadima's hand right where mine touched the metal. Her hard, calloused hands would pat mine, and she'd say the short prayer she often said, *"Rang tamaasaa pooran aasaa kabeh na biaapai chintaa."* Which meant something like "joy and happiness be yours, may your wishes come true and worries never trouble you."

Worries. They always troubled me.

I leaned against the pillar Sara had chosen during orientation, inhaling the diesel from the buses, the floor polish from the open office doors, and the antiseptic smell of the freshly cleaned classrooms, and waited for the buses to arrive. Usually I'd be worried about the amount of carcinogens I was breathing in, but right then I actually couldn't get enough of that first-day-of-school smell.

I busied myself by watching familiar faces file past.

Sara started taking the bus last year when her mom began working part-time. She used to say I was so lucky because I walked, but after a month on the bus, she decided that the bus was the best way to get to school. The older kids talked about scary movies we weren't allowed to watch and rumors about the eighth-grade dances. I smiled now, remembering how Sara would listen to their conversations and tell me about them as we walked to class.

As the buses started to pull in, I patted at the lemon juice above my lip. Between the lemon juice and the few strokes of mascara, I hoped it would be enough to disguise the hair for today until I could come up with a better plan.

"Karma!" called a familiar voice.

Ruthie jumped down each step of bus forty-two. She ran to me and wrapped her arms around my waist. I gave her a quick squeeze, glancing over her head to find Sara.

But I saw Lacy first. Well, first I saw sparkly blue shoes and then the matching sparkly clip in her hair. Of course. I should have remembered that Lacy would be taking the same bus as Sara, but somehow I had expected her to arrive in a chauffeured car with paparazzi tailing her. It actually struck me as kind of funny that she walked off an ordinary, yellow, rusting school bus.

Sara filed off the bus behind Lacy. She saw me and waved. I pushed off the pillar, keeping one hand in Ruthie's.

Lacy glanced up but pretended she didn't see me. I knew she was pretending, because Sara and I had invented that look together last year to use when we were alone in the hall and a teacher walked toward us. It was a way to avoid having to look at or talk to someone.

All you do is look down at your shoes or socks and pretend you have to fix something. Then by the time you look up, the other person would have walked past you.

It *had* to be "the look" because how could she have to fix anything on a brand-new pair of sparkly shoes? If Sara had told Lacy about the look when they were together last night, Sara must have told her other secrets too. Pinpricks of uneasiness washed over me.

"Hey," Sara said. "I didn't know if you'd be waiting here."

"Of course." I forced a smile onto my face, because she would've known I'd be waiting if she'd called me over the past two days.

"Sissy," Ruthie said, tugging at Sara's backpack strap. "I don't want to go. Can I go to your class with Karma?"

"Ugh. I knew this would happen. If you don't go, Mom will have to drive you tomorrow."

Sara's eyes begged me for help. "Sorry, guys. I have to walk Ruthie to the crossing guard."

Sara was the Oreo filling that bonded Lacy and me. Without Sara, Lacy and I weren't anything but two black discs with nothing holding us together. I flushed at the memory of the entire Oreo incident in Sara's basement. Before I could come up with an excuse to tag along with Sara, Derek ran by and yelled, "'Stache Attack!"

Kids from other buses walked around me, and a few laughed at Derek and looked at me, puzzled. They didn't get the joke.

Yet.

Chapter Twelve

I pulled on my backpack straps and held my breath as I walked toward Ms. Hillary and my classroom. Just before I reached the classroom door, I looked over my shoulder at Mrs. Clark's room across the hall. The kids were drawing on the board and sitting on their desks waiting for the bell. As I got closer to my classroom, something about Ms. Hillary's scowl told me she'd be the kind of teacher who would make us play "educational" games on party days, while Mrs. Clark's class would be drinking soda and popping balloons.

When I walked into the classroom, everyone sat at or stood near a desk, with their bag on the floor next to them. There were no assigned seats, but Lacy stood by some desks in the back row, talking with Kate and Emma in a way that made it clear she had assigned those seats for her and her followers. She had followed Derek to the classroom, without giving me so much as a glance.

I didn't know where to sit. I'd never had to choose where to sit before. Sara and I always just walked into the classroom and sat. But now I didn't know which desk Sara would choose. Was she a Lacy follower?

"Oh my gosh," Sara said, walking up behind me.

I didn't bother to stifle my sigh when I heard Sara's voice.

"That took forever. Ruthie started crying, so I had to stay until one of the teacher's aides came." Sara blew at the short strands of hair that she'd left loose around her face.

"She'll be okay. Remember how much you cried on the first day?"

"Ugh. Please do not remind me." Sara rolled her eyes and shook her head, but she had a smile on her face. "Do you smell that?" she asked. "They must have used some heavy-duty lemon cleaner in here."

I reached up to my mouth and rubbed the sides like I had an itch. My lip felt sticky. "Yeah. That stuff is really strong." I needed to wash the lemon juice off, the first chance I got. I put my backpack on the desk next to me and reached in to get the eraser and folder Mom had given me that morning. "My mom—"

"Sara," Lacy called. "Kate and Emma wanna read that article. Bring it here. "

"Yeah, sure." Sara pulled her bag up onto her shoulder and looked over at me. "Come sit with us."

I turned my head to the back of the room, where Lacy sat. She whispered to Kate and Emma. Their eyes darted back at me and they giggled. Lacy put her finger over her lip in a 'Stache Attack sign.

"Actually, why don't you sit up here? With me?" I asked.

"*Sara*, the article," Lacy said.

"Okay," Sara said. "Let me give this stupid magazine to Lacy. Just a minute."

I kept my bag on the desk. I tried not to move it too much, so the dal wouldn't spill.

"Hey," David said, walking toward me. Well, David shuffled more than walked. One leg was longer than the other, and he tended to drag the shorter one even though his shoe had a thicker bottom to even his legs out. My mom had tried to explain to me in kindergarten that David had been born premature and had been really sick as a baby. His name was always on honor roll with mine, but his body and maturity never seemed to catch up with the rest of us. Still, he had been off-limits to real teasing since kindergarten.

"My bag is there." For someone so small, he had a really loud, squeaky voice. He pointed at a blue backpack on the other side of the desk.

"Sorry." I grabbed my bag and moved over a row.

"Karma's stealing David's seat," Tom said. "'Stache Attack, dude!" Tom put his finger over his mouth.

Maybe it was just me, but the room suddenly felt quieter and a million degrees hotter. Tom might have been making fun of David or me. I couldn't tell.

I wanted to find Sara's eyes. Instead I found Lacy gawking at David with that freaked-out look everyone makes when they meet him for the first time.

Last year he missed three months of school for another surgery and came back with a medical waist pack. It looked like a normal waist pack Daddy would wear on vacation, but it had a tube attached and a bag full of pee inside. It'd been weird for the first few weeks after he came back to school. We were all worried about bumping into him or hurting him, and making his pee pack explode, but now we hardly noticed it.

Lacy, on the other hand, let out a loud, "Eww. What's wrong with him?"

David smiled and nodded proudly as he explained his pee pack. He was the only kid I knew who didn't worry about nicknames. I had to give him credit for being so proud.

Someone cleared their throat behind me. "You sitting there?"

I turned around. Ginny, a.k.a. Guinea Pig, stood next to the desk. At least she could directly blame her parents for the torture bestowed upon her, since they'd chosen a hard-to-read name. I mean, "Karma" might not be the most common name, but at least its mispronunciation can't be confused with a furry rodent. And if just one kid mispronouncing "Ginny" as "Guinea" in first grade could brand you with a nickname for life, what would 'Stache Attack become once it caught on?

"Well?" she asked.

I realized I'd left my backpack on the desk I'd

saved for Sara. But Sara still stood at the back of the classroom, hunched over a magazine with Kate and Emma. I couldn't go back there with lemon-smelling clumps of hair on my face and join Sara. And, from the looks of it, Sara didn't seem to be missing me at all.

"It's yours." I grabbed my things and slipped into the desk in front of Ginny.

Ms. Hillary didn't waste any time. She passed out a list of class rules—twenty, to be exact—and then she gave us our locker assignments, which were alphabetical. Karma Khullar landed between Lacy Jenkins on the left and Ginny Meyers on the right.

We filed into the hall to empty our bags into our lockers. Ms. Hillary hovered behind us, making sure we could all figure out our combinations.

Sara and Emma laughed as they put up mirrors and other locker-decorating stuff. I'd seen those locker kit things when Daddy had taken me school shopping, but I'd rolled my eyes. I didn't think anyone really bought them. Especially not Sara.

Watching the other girls laugh and decorate their lockers made me want to have someone to talk to as well. I tried to smile at Ginny, but she was busy stacking her notebooks by size. She also added a couple of recycling magnets and a peace sign magnet to the inside of her locker door.

I opened my mouth to tell her that her magnets were nice, but Ms. Hillary cleared her throat behind me.

"Let's not waste any time, please."

I lifted my folders plus the one for Sara out of my bag. Yellow dal dripped off the bottom and splattered onto my leg. I quickly wiped it with my hand, hoping no one would notice. Some of the dal had leaked out and formed a small watery, yellow puddle at the bottom of my backpack. I held the tiffin up to figure out how to clean it.

"What is that?" Lacy inched away from me. She eyed my tiffin like I held a dead rat in my hands instead of my lunch.

"It's my . . . um, lunch?" I hated that she made me question everything.

"Looks like baby poop. Yuck." Lacy held her hand over her nose and slammed her locker closed.

I'd thought the tiffin would make me less worried about things, but instead it turned out to be one more thing Lacy could make fun of. Then again, it was just my lunch. It couldn't possibly be worse than 'Stache Attack.

A few girls around her giggled. Lacy smiled at her triumph, and she grabbed on to their arms, skirting around me as if dal was contagious.

"Hurry up," Ms. Hillary called to David and me, the only two still unpacking our bags.

I tried to push my tiffin into the bottom of the locker, in front of my books. The locker wasn't deep enough. I couldn't chance putting the tiffin on top of my books, what if it leaked again? Sweat formed on my arms and the backs of my knees.

"Is there a problem, Karma?" Ms. Hillary asked, her shoes clomp-clomping toward me.

"My lunch doesn't fit."

"Hmm. Follow me with your . . . your . . ." She paused with her finger pointing at the tiffin.

"Tiffin."

"Yes, of course, *tiffin*." She said it slowly like the word was uncomfortable in her mouth. Which, I guess it probably was. I must have been the only person outside India who carried a stainless steel tiffin to school as my lunch box. That should have been my first sign that I'd made a mistake bringing it to school.

I followed Ms. Hillary into the classroom. Everyone's eyes followed us curiously as we crossed the room in a spotlight of stares. I clutched the tiffin tightly in my left hand, trying to hide it against my leg. Ms. Hillary walked all the way to the back of the classroom and opened the storage closet. It smelled of dust and fresh paper, a very *school* smell. The closet walls were lined with small shelves that were filled with reams of paper and extra markers and erasers for the board.

Ms. Hillary pushed a box of paper aside to make room on the nearest shelf for the tiffin. "That ought to be fine."

"Thanks."

"Just keep your lunch in here. It's always unlocked."

I put the tiffin on the shelf and walked back to my seat. I prayed to Babaji that none of the dal had leaked onto my skirt, leaving a yellow baby-poop stain.

I opened my notebook to the middle of the pages, where the corners weren't stained yellow, and grasped my newly sharpened pencil so tight that my thumbnail dug into my pointer finger. It was the only way to keep the tears of embarrassment behind my eyes from spilling out.

Chapter Thirteen

When the bell rang, we went across the hall to Mrs. Clark's for social studies. Even though we switched teachers and classrooms for each subject, we stayed together as a class. I'd liked the idea of sticking together because it'd be less likely for me to get lost, but having Lacy, Tom, and Derek trail me all day didn't really put me at ease.

Mrs. Clark stood in the front of the classroom with her hands clasped, bouncing on her toes. "I'm excited to share with you what we've got in store for this year. As was mentioned at orientation, you sixth graders have an opportunity to get more involved here at Holly Creek Middle School. We're looking for ideas to help you learn beyond the classroom.

Suggestion boxes have been placed in each home-room, where you can anonymously drop your ideas to help make learning engaging."

"You mean we can put stuff in there like going to McDonald's?" Tom asked.

Mrs. Clark smiled patiently. "Well, if that would help you, let's say, in math, or health, and you could give a valid reason for it, then sure."

"What about going to the mall?" Lacy asked.

"Yeah, or the park?" someone else said.

"You guys are kind of missing the point," Mrs. Clark said. "Let's think bigger. For example, we are going to be discussing early civilizations. We'll be learning how they survived and planted their own food and made their own clothing. So, where could we go to discover more about this?"

"The zoo!" Tom shouted.

"A farm," Kate said.

"We could camp," Sara said.

Just hearing Sara's voice sent a jolt through my body. I thought it would be comforting and reassuring. Instead it sent a zap of static electricity that cut through me.

She'd sat in the back with Lacy in homeroom even when Ms. Hillary had asked if anyone wished to move. Well, the likes of Lacy wouldn't get the better of me.

"We could start a garden," I said.

"That's great. I love those ideas. Well, the zoo was a stretch," Mrs. Clark said. "Camping is a very good idea." She smiled at Sara.

I looked over at Sara, proud that Mrs. Clark had complimented her. Behind Sara, Lacy shoved her finger over her mouth in a 'Stache Attack.

Mrs. Clark turned to me. "And, Karma, what a great idea about a garden. That is really thinking big. Not only would a garden give us hands-on learning experience, but it would also give us an opportunity to give back, either to the community or to our school. The suggestions you place in the boxes can also be for after-school groups and clubs that help organize learning opportunities outside of school. That's the kind of big ideas I want all of you to brainstorm tonight. Obviously, I said this is anonymous, but I do want to challenge all of you to come up with one 'big idea' to consider putting in your homeroom suggestion box tomorrow."

A "big idea." If I'd been able to come up with a big idea, I'd have been mustache-less and still have a best friend. So how was I supposed to come up with an idea for class when I couldn't even think of a good idea for getting rid of my mustache?

Even though it'd been empty all summer, the lunchroom still smelled like sweat, basketballs, and leftover meat loaf. The entire room overflowed with kids and noise.

The tables were nearly full, and I couldn't spot my class. I'd left a couple of minutes after everyone else because of my tiffin being in the storage closet. Then I'd stopped off in the bathroom to wash off the lemon juice. It had hardened and made the hair clump at the edges of my mouth. Once I rinsed it and dried it with a paper towel, it wasn't sticky, just red from the rubbing. So I waited a couple of minutes for the red to go away.

Looking around the bathroom, I considered staying and eating my lunch in there, but it would be impossible to open up my tiffin and eat unless I sat on the floor—and no way would I ever eat on the bathroom floor, even if, statistically speaking, there were less germs in a public bathroom than on your toothbrush at home. Maybe a sandwich would have been doable by standing and eating, but not soupy dal and chapatis.

I held the tiffin to my side, trying to hide it behind me, but when you're walking through the middle of a huge open room, there is no behind or beside. Everything is visible to everyone. I tried to keep my head down and use only my eyes to look up—a way of walking and sitting I'd been getting used to today. I didn't want to bump into anyone, but I also didn't want to catch anyone's eye.

"Hey, Khullar, that your shaving kit?" Tom asked.

"Nice one," Derek said, slapping him a high five.

Well, at least I'd found my class. There weren't really assigned seats at lunch now that we were in middle school, but maybe because it was the first day, most of the classes kind of stuck together.

The gap between Emma and Kate disappeared as I moved closer. All around the table, gaps disappeared. I looked for Sara but didn't notice her anywhere. There was an empty spot beside Derek, but I didn't dare.

The only other spots available were by Ginny and David. I held my head high and walked right past Lacy to sit next to Ginny at the table behind Lacy's.

I did my best to put the tiffin down gently, but it still managed to hit the table with a clunk.

Ginny looked up, an arm's length away on my right. I smiled, but she just turned back to stare at her sandwich. Across the table David slurped chocolate milk from his thermos. He smiled, showing all his teeth, not bothering to stop drinking, so little dribbles of brown milk leaked from the sides of his mouth and dripped off his chin. His teeth were so crowded in his narrow mouth that it looked like they were fighting to escape.

Those crammed-together teeth made me self-conscious of my own, even though they were probably the one feature I had that didn't stress me out. Still, I smiled back at him with my lips tightly closed. I busied myself with unclasping the handle of the tiffin so I could separate the two bowls. The smell of dal calmed me slightly. If I closed my eyes, I could imagine I was at home. I tore off a piece of chapati and dipped it into the yellow dal.

"Eww."

At the other end of Lacy's table, Kate threw a wrapper from her store-bought snack at a grinning Derek.

"That's so gross," Emma echoed.

"I swear I didn't fart," Derek said, throwing wrappers back at them.

Lacy pushed herself forward, practically lying across the table to find where the smell was coming from.

"Eww! 'Stache Attack is eating her own throw-up!" she yelled, tapping Kate on the shoulder. I bit down hard on my chapati and swallowed the bite whole. Lacy's eyes had a glint like the sun shining on an icicle. She'd said that on purpose. She'd said it to remind me about Supremo's.

"Oh, gross!" Kate and Emma said at the same time.

"Up-chuck! Up-chuck! Up-chuck!" Tom chanted, pounding the table.

I covered my food with my arms, not sure if I wanted to protect it or hide it. I didn't even know why everyone was making such a big deal about my lunch. I wasn't the only one with ethnic food. Yeji brought kimchi and rice cakes each day except taco day.

Kids from surrounding tables craned their necks to get a good look at my dal. No one wanted to be left out. Everyone wanted to claim they'd witnessed a girl eating her own vomit.

Mrs. Clark ran toward our table. "Is someone sick?"

"I'm gonna be sick!" Derek covered his mouth and puffed out his cheeks. "BLAH. BLAH. BLECH." He fake puked into his hands and put it in front of my face. The heat from his sweaty palm made me want to gag. It was so close, I could count the tiny spit bubbles that had landed on his hand.

The lunchroom shrunk. There were so many faces laughing and gawking and staring. This must have been the nightmare dentists have, sitting in a room, staring at gaping mouths full of half-eaten food and bits stuck between back teeth.

Heat rose up my body and made the backs of my knees sticky.

"That's enough," Mrs. Clark said, resting her hand on my shoulder. "Everyone back to your seats."

Sara arrived next to Lacy with a tray as the other kids were slowly going back toward their tables, still giggling and whispering and pointing. A few put their fingers in a 'Stache Attack sign.

"It's wonderful that Karma brings such delicious food for lunch." Mrs. Clark leaned down and smiled right at me.

If I could have just stared at her warm, brown eyes and her smile and ignored the laughing and jeering all around me, then I would have smiled too. But she probably only smiled because she didn't have to clean up barf, and no matter how nice she was being, it wasn't enough to block out the noise.

She patted my shoulder before walking away.

"Oh, that's so delicious!" Tom said in an exaggerated girly voice, dabbing the sides of his mouth with an invisible napkin. "If you're the bearded lady!"

I didn't bother to lift my eyes to figure out who laughed or who didn't. Lacy would probably tell Sara everything that had just happened. I couldn't believe Sara had chosen Lacy over me in homeroom and now in the lunchroom. Now would have been a good time for Sara to stick up for me. But she still said nothing.

Even though I'd only had a bite, I closed the tiffin and waited for the bell. A few minutes later everyone started to empty their trays and throw away their garbage.

Lacy walked toward the trash cans, scrunching up her brown paper lunch bag. "What's this?" she asked, gesturing at the table strewn with my tiffin, David's random plastic containers, and

Ginny's insulated lunch box. "The lunch box group? Starting a new club, Kar?" She tossed her bag into the bin.

I opened my mouth to say something, but it just stayed open like that. Completely empty—exactly how I felt. I felt open, exposed, and without all the things that had once filled me. Like the deer Sara's dad had once shot and cut open right down the center to hang from a tree in her backyard. That's how I felt right then. Gutted.

Ginny cleared her throat next to me. It was the first noise she'd made since I'd sat next to her. "It's green to reuse, and don't you know that *green* is in?" She zipped her lunch bag closed with a flourish.

I sat up straight and stared at Ginny with awe that she could think of anything to say.

Lacy must have been more shocked than me, because she stood still, her mouth squeezed into a pucker, looking a few sparkles short of a tube of glitter glue. She grabbed Kate's arm and stomped off toward the bathroom.

"Thanks," I said, still staring at Ginny in awe.

"For what?" she asked. "I care about saving the earth, not saving you. Come on, David."

Her words stung worse than Lacy's or Tom's

insults. I guess because I knew Ginny was right. Lacy and Tom were mean, but Ginny, well, she had no reason to care about me or to defend me. I'd never given her much thought before today. I'd even referred to her as "Guinea Pig" in my head. Now here I was, sitting next to her and expecting her to stand up for me.

My brain was a kaleidoscope of thoughts— little shapes bumping around and knocking into other shapes, making a big mess. Only, instead of being beautiful from every angle, it was confusing. "'Stache Attack" had caught on. My tiffin lunch had just about caused a riot. I had no idea if Sara was even my friend anymore. I had no idea if I had *any* friends, since not even Ginny wanted anything to do with me.

In order to survive middle school, I had to do something. And now I had more than just a mustache to worry about.

Chapter Fourteen

An embarrassment-burn stung my face as I put my tiffin back into the storage closet. I had a few minutes before the next bell, and I needed each second. Everything at lunch had happened in such a blur. As I thought about it, I felt like a marshmallow left in the microwave about five seconds too long. Tears formed behind my eyes, and my mind replayed the scene over and over.

Derek's spit-sprayed hand in my face and the gawking cackles of the rest of the lunchroom played on the backs of my eyelids whenever I closed my eyes. No matter how much I willed it to go away or how many times I tried to calm myself by repeating *Satnam Waheguru*, the sting stayed.

There was a rustle in the classroom, so I took a

deep breath and came out of the storage closet. I didn't want anyone to think I'd stood in there crying.

"Oh. Hey, Karma." Sara stood by her desk with a binder in her arms. "I forgot this under my desk earlier. I can't seem to do anything right today. Somebody should write a first-day manual, huh? I had no idea the lunch line would take so long. I had like five minutes to eat, and by then everyone was going crazy and the food was cold. I should have packed like you did."

I forced out a laugh, afraid I'd throw myself at her in a hug and cry to her if I didn't.

Sara opened her binder. "Hey, and I almost forgot to give this to you." She pulled out a copy of *Teen Bop*. "Here's that article about a natural scrub for facial hair."

My skin tingled with embarrassment even though we were the only ones around.

"Um. Thanks."

We had walked quietly to our lockers before I asked her what had been growing inside me for days, growing so big, it pushed out and I couldn't stop it any longer. "So, is Lacy your new best friend?"

Sara stood in front of her locker. "She's not my

best friend. I've only known her a couple of days. You'd like her if you got to know her."

"Like her? I don't even understand why *you* like her."

Sara stopped spinning her lock. "Look, I know she's not exactly super nice, but she's just trying to make friends. It's normal. There was an article about it a couple of pages after the scrub article. New girls feel the need to make others notice them, and being opinionated is just one of those ways. Don't take it so personally."

"But it *is* personal. She's not going around ruining anyone else's life."

"Jeesh, Karma. Why do you always have to be so dramatic? She's not *ruining* your life."

"She started 'Stache Attack."

"No. Derek and Tom started it."

That was true. Instead of arguing I ran my thumbnail along the gap of my locker door.

Sara slammed her locker and turned to me "Lacy is in our class, she lives across the street from me, she's new—I mean, what do you want me to do? Ignore her?"

"No, I just wish you weren't so BFF with her, that's all."

"You and I've been friends forever. It's always just the two of us. It doesn't hurt to have more friends."

I shrugged.

Sara sighed. "This isn't the third grade anymore, Karma."

She was right, of course, but I sure wished that all I had to worry about was finishing my math work first so I could get a turn sitting in the reading beanbag at the back of our third-grade classroom.

Right now Sara look like old Sara, with her fingernail polish already chipped and picked at, because that's what she does when she's nervous. But under all the things I knew so well about her, a part of her I'd never known existed had emerged. Like lifting up a rock and finding it squirming with an entire miniature world. She wasn't the old Sara who had once kicked a boy in the shins with her cowgirl boots when he kept pulling my braids. She'd turned into the new Sara who chose to sit with Lacy in homeroom and ignore that 'Stache Attack was happening.

"Fine," I said. "You want to be friends with her? Be friends with her, but don't expect me to be friends with either of you."

"That's *really* mature. Maybe you should read Zendaya's guest post on friendship. Page thirty-six."

Sara stomped off toward class, leaving me alone in the hallway.

This wasn't one of those arguments that would blow over and be forgotten in a couple of days. Lacy had brought along a Californian-style seismic shift and stuck it right smack-dab in between Sara and me.

I stood at my desk, stacking and restacking my books, trying to look busy. I didn't want Sara to think I missed talking to her.

The bus bell rang, and the classroom emptied. The tide of bodies in the hallway swept all the craziness out the door and onto the buses. For the first time in the entire school day, mostly quiet surrounded me. No teacher talking or giving instructions, no one sharpening a pencil or clicking a pen or tapping on their desk; yet my ears still buzzed with the things that had happened.

Ginny, David, two other boys, and I were the only ones left in the classroom. Ginny helped David with his backpack. The other boys played something with cards. I stood at my desk, and the buzzing in my ears got worse. I didn't even hear the walker bell. Everyone filed out of the room, so I followed.

Ginny walked ahead of me. I wanted to catch up to her and say something, but I needed something to say first. There was no point walking next to her in an awkward silence. Times like this, I wished I would write down the clever conversation starters that entered my brain before I fell asleep. Then I could carry around my little notebook and never have to endure any awkwardness.

I slowed down, giving myself time to come up with something smart but not too smart. Funny was out—I could never pull off funny, not on purpose anyway. Then I remembered her locker magnets and jogged after her.

"Hey, Ginny," I called.

She stopped and turned around, holding the door open.

"I just wanted to say that I really like your recycling magnets. You know, the ones in your locker."

"Yeah. I know the ones," Ginny said.

A laugh echoed in her voice, but when I lifted my eyes to check, I found a real smile.

I took a big inhale of the outside air. "Also, what you said to Lacy . . . that was . . . hilarious." I fidgeted with the straps of my backpack to hide the burn of my cheeks, which were probably chili red.

"Well, it's true. Green is in, and more people should bring reusable lunch boxes. What goes around comes around. Be nice to the earth, and it'll be nice to you."

That reminded me of something Dadima liked to say: "Your actions start a trail of reactions." Which she said explained karma way better than "What goes around comes around" because it's more about what we do than what others do to us.

"Maybe you should suggest that as your big idea for the suggestion box," I said.

Ginny cocked her head at me. "That's not a bad idea. BYOB—'bring your own bag.' Like at the grocery store."

Her smile softened the hard lines that usually etched her mouth. I wondered if this was how she looked at home, where no one called her "Guinea Pig."

We were quiet as we made our way up the hill. This simple chat with Ginny lightened my mood, despite my backpack being weighed down with every textbook from my locker. Daddy had asked me to bring them home, like he did every year. He wanted to ensure my education was "well-rounded." By that, he meant he would go online and to the university library to supplement my education with long lectures and handouts.

Unfortunately, none of that knowledge came in handy now. I mean, if Daddy really wanted me to be "well-rounded," maybe he should have made *Teen Bop* magazine required reading. After all, it had an article on how to scrub away a mustache with some sugar, and advice on friendship, both things I desperately needed help with.

Is this how everyone figured stuff out? I might have asked Mom once upon a time, but Sara had been right about one thing. We weren't in the third grade anymore. Not only had Mom been too busy with work, but I shouldn't have had to ask my mom to help me. I should have been able to do this myself.

Ginny waved and turned down her street, leaving me with the echo of her words bouncing around in my head: "What goes around comes around."

Maybe I was getting what I deserved?

Maybe this was my karma.

Chapter Fifteen

'm home," I called as I walked through the door. I let my backpack drop to the floor in the kitchen.

For the first time since I'd woken up that morning, I felt like I could take a deep breath, knowing not a single person at home knew anything about 'Stache Attack.

"Daddy?" I poked my head into his study, but it was empty. I quickly grabbed the tiffin from my bag and took several bites of dal, because I didn't want Daddy to ask why I hadn't eaten it at school. I couldn't bear to dump it out at school because Dadima used to tell me that throwing away perfectly good food was like telling Babaji to stop blessing you with good things.

I left the tiffin in the sink so Daddy would know

I'd eaten most of it, and went upstairs to find him.

He wasn't there. Nobody was home. But Daddy was *always* home. I checked for a note. Again, nothing.

Every force in the cosmos came together to remind me that nothing was the same as it had been last year. Last year Mom would have been home, or she'd have left a note next to a snack on the counter. But that was only once, when Kiran got sick at school and she had to pick him up.

That day last year had been the last time I'd been home alone. My body did that weird twitchy thing that happens when I drink an entire cup of masala tea. To calm down I went around to all the windows downstairs and closed the curtains. I hated myself for doing it, for being such a baby.

It took two granola bars and several peeks out the closed curtains to convince myself that Daddy had probably gotten tied up at the grocery store and that Kiran would be home any minute from school, before I could calm down enough to stop fidgeting and pacing.

I grabbed my backpack and went up to my room. Sitting at my desk, surrounded by my familiar walls, made me feel less alone. Only Ms. Hillary had given us homework, so I reached into my bag to pull out my English book. I'd keep the rest of my textbooks in my bag until Daddy asked for them later. The sticky pages of *Teen Bop* stuck to the back of my English book.

Just when I'd managed to smother my panic about being home alone, the memory of fighting with Sara and the words "facial hair" replayed in my head. No way would a stupid magazine be able to help me. I'd already rubbed my face raw like a crazy monk, and the lemon juice had been a bust. How would a magazine that featured smooth-skinned girls do me any good?

Then again, Horrible Histories was totally ancient, and things had changed a lot. *And* maybe those girls had smooth skin because they used the sugar scrub. It wouldn't hurt to just read the article.

Tingles of embarrassment spread across my face as I opened the magazine. Even though I was home alone, I couldn't help but keep it hidden in my English book.

I skimmed the articles until I reached the page with the recipe for the sugar scrub. You had to mix sugar, water, and lemon juice and rub it on your face before bed. Yeah, right. I'd already been rubbing, AND I'd used lemon juice this morning. Adding sugar wasn't going to magically make my mustache disappear.

At least it didn't suggest I shave it off, like Kiran teased me about. Sikhs don't cut their hair. I might not be a typical Sikh or even a 100 percent one. Mom took us to church on Easter and Christmas, and Daddy brought us to the gurdwara on Diwali and Vaisakhi. Still, Daddy didn't let Mom cut my hair. She took me for trims now and again but never let them cut more than an inch or two. Kiran cut his when he turned five because kids at his kindergarten called him a girl. Daddy still kept his hair long, but wrapped it up under a turban so it wasn't very obvious.

If I didn't come up with another solution, I'd end up twisting and tucking my mustache into a turban the way Daddy did with his beard. Daddy rolled his beard under and tucked it up on either side of his face to keep it from hanging down. He said it was too hot and itchy, but Dadima would tsk. She said summers in India were even hotter than summers here, and Dadaji managed to keep his beard loose until he died at eighty years old.

I looked up from the article and right to the

pamphlet I'd grabbed out of the recycling the other day. *Your Karma, Your Life*. I pulled the paper off my mirror and unfolded it so I could read the entire thing.

> *A talk by Dr. Gurwinder Singh.*
> *Come on the 23rd of September at 7 p.m.*
> *for an enlightening discussion about*
> *karma through the scriptures of Gurbani.*

When Ginny had brought up the whole "what goes around comes around" thing on our walk home, I'd been half thinking that karma was messing with me. Now, looking back at the entire summer—with my mustache, Daddy losing his job, Mom becoming super busy, Kiran being grumpy, me getting called 'Stache Attack, and Sara and me getting all weird—maybe it wasn't such a crazy idea. I mean, in books kids got superpowers when they turned twelve or thirteen. Maybe in real life you got a dose of karma served to you.

I thought that there must be a way to turn bad karma good. Things had already gotten so out of control, I couldn't wait the two weeks until the twenty-third to figure it out.

Below, the garage door shifted and complained as it opened. I shoved *Teen Bop* back into my school bag and ran down the stairs.

Kiran barged through the door at the same time I got to the kitchen. His backpack hung off one shoulder, and his hair hid half his face. Daddy came in right behind him, waving a paper.

"This isn't over, young man," Daddy yelled.

"You never listen," Kiran yelled back.

Every muscle in my body pulled back in surprise.

"I don't have to listen. It's all written down here on paper!" Daddy poked the paper furiously with his finger.

"Fine!" Kiran didn't wait for Daddy's response. He stomped up the stairs and slammed his door. His footsteps paced back and forth in his room, making the floorboards creak. Daddy stared at the paper in his hand and shook his head. Then he turned to me and acted surprised to see me standing there.

"It's four thirty?" He rubbed the face of his watch like he wanted to erase time. He crunched the paper in his fist and stormed into his study. He left the door open a sliver, so the noise of him slamming drawers and pounding on the keyboard still seeped out.

All of this was an unspoken sign that dinner was my duty. It's not that Daddy would tell me I had to. If I looked in the fridge, I could find leftovers, and Mom would be able to whip something up when she got home, but strained silence always made me feel like I hovered on the edge of a cliff, about to fall off with a single gust of wind. Making dinner or cleaning up kept me busy and moving and, I hoped, safe from collateral damage.

I grabbed some eggs, tomatoes, and butter from the fridge and went to the stove. Omelets were my specialty. Mostly because it's all I knew how to make from my two years of Brownies. I had everything in the pan when Mom walked through the door.

"That smells yummy," she said, patting my shoulder. "Why are you making dinner? Where's your father?"

"In the study."

"That doesn't sound good."

Her eyes went from Daddy's study door to the ceiling where Kiran's room was.

"Your first day of school went well?" she asked, giving me a quick hug.

I nodded. I wished I could just tell her the truth, that school was awful and weird and I had a mustache problem and most likely terrible karma to top it all off. But her eyes watched Daddy's door. It really wasn't the best time to dump out all my problems.

"Let me have a word with your father, and then I'll help you with a salad." She patted my back again and walked toward Daddy's study.

I had chopped the lettuce and grated the carrots and radishes for the salad by the time they finally came out of the study. It had felt good to chop those vegetables to teeny tiny bits. So good, I didn't mind that no one had helped me.

Daddy sat down at the table and scowled as I brought the food over.

"Bring the hot sauce and some char," he said. "I can't believe I'm eating eggs and salad for dinner. What do I look like? A rabbit?"

Daddy always got grumpy over food when he was in a bad mood. I just nodded as I got the spicy pickles and hot sauce from the fridge.

"I'll change and get Kiran. Then we can all eat," Mom said with a smile that forced the dimple on her cheek to appear but couldn't make her eyes happy.

A quiet settled over dinner that made every *tink* of my fork sound too loud. Daddy's mood shriveled my thoughts of wanting to ask him about the talk at the temple.

In a way I didn't mind that Kiran's problems overshadowed mine—I didn't have to talk about any of them. But a small part of me was stung because I did want to tell *someone.* I would normally call Sara to complain, but that wasn't a possibility, considering that my problems had expanded beyond just a mustache to include her. Mom had work to worry about, and obviously I couldn't just bring the topic of my fight with Sara or my mustache up to Daddy.

Dadima would have understood. She liked to tell me that Sikh girls had to be a lamb on the outside and a lion on the inside. Strong and determined. I didn't feel either right now.

Chapter Sixteen

Dadima's box sat on the top shelf of the linen closet upstairs. It held a few of her most special keepsakes, like a prayer book, her favorite *chunni* that she used to wear over her head when she prayed, and her wedding bangles—things she'd had in the same box under her bed while she lived with us. I knew everything in there, because I used to go through the box every day during the weeks after she died. Then I realized that all the opening and closing of the box made her smell disappear. So I stuck it up high and left it, hoping it would be full of her smell again.

I tiptoed across the hall to the closet, trying not to listen to Daddy lecture Kiran or Mom's muffled voice. I pulled out the step stool so I could reach the top shelf and grab the box, and held the lid closed with my thumbs. The rumble of Daddy's voice drifted up the steps as I slipped back into my room and closed my door behind me.

I inhaled slowly once I took the lid off the box. Dadima's scent lingered faintly and sent a surge of memories through me.

The smoky, woodsy smell of chapatis cooking.

Cardamom, fresh and minty on her breath.

The yellowed skin of her thumb and pointer finger from turmeric.

The soft *plinks* of her bangles as she moved around the house.

I grabbed the prayer book and quickly pushed the lid back onto the box before any more of her smell could escape. The prayer book was only a little bigger than my hand. It was a hardcover, but it felt comfortable clutched between my fingers. Dadima's bookmark was still stuck randomly in the book. I let the book fall open to the page and started to read the English translation on the right side.

> *This precious human life is a reward for*
> *my past actions, but without wisdom, it*

is wasted. Tell me, without worship of
the Lord, of what use are mansions and
thrones like those of King Indra?

I had no idea who King Indra was, and mansions didn't sound so bad to me, but I got the impression that I shouldn't want them.

The next part read:

The Naam lives within the minds of
those who worship the Lord. Those who
are separated from the Naam shall never
find peace. Many come and go; they die,
and die again, and are reincarnated.
Without understanding, they are useless
and wander.

I let those words tumble inside my head like clothes in a dryer. They mixed together into non-sense, but at times fell on top of each other in a way that made me wonder if somehow I had something to do with this. If "this precious human life is a reward for my past actions" was true, then maybe my past actions weren't very good. Maybe they were really horrible. Maybe I had been a hot-water girl in my past life! What if I deserved this mustache because I'd been mean in my past?

Well, I guess I was getting what was coming around. It was a karma curse. Karma's karma curse.

Those who are separated from the Naam shall never find peace. I needed to be with the Naam, with God. I read through more of Dadima's prayer book in Punjabi, not because the Punjabi was easier to understand than the English but because it was nice to let the words work parts of my mouth the way my mouth works when I'm chewing gum, ready to blow a bubble. Reading in Punjabi was easy. Understanding it was the hard part. The sections that were too confusing, I cheated and read the English translation.

After just reciting a few prayers from the book, I already felt closer to the Naam. If I did suffer from a karma curse, the first thing I needed to do was earn some major karma points.

I turned the page to a list of vices to avoid. As I read through them, I started to think of all the ways I wasn't really a very good person.

For example, Covetousness and Greed. I'd wanted Sara as my BFF and no one else, and I hated that she wanted other people as her BFF. I'd been a pretty selfish friend, and now I'd lost Sara.

Attachment to Things of This World was the next vice. I didn't really think I was attached to much, but it did bother me that the car door squeaked and that our house only had one bathroom upstairs for us all to use in the morning.

I'd thought Pride was only a problem for someone like Lacy, but I had cared when everyone had laughed at 'Stache Attack and at my lunch.

The last vice was Anger. I imagined the day at the pool when Lacy had pointed out my mustache and Derek and Tom had invented 'Stache Attack, and then today when I had fought with Sara after lunch. A small twinge of heat stirred in my chest.

There wasn't a single vice I could say I didn't have. No wonder I had a mustache!

There weren't any rules that I could find for earning karma points, so I made up my own. In my head it made sense. I'd get points for not getting angry or prideful or having any of the vices. But if I did have these things, I'd lose points.

I had no idea how many points I'd need to clean up my karma and break this curse. Once I could get to the place where I didn't need to think so much about karma, maybe my mustache would start to disappear and my family could go back to normal. No more fighting, no more tension.

Trying to get myself to not be angry or prideful or jealous might take a while, but I had an idea for the school suggestion box that just might help.

Chapter Seventeen

Before breakfast the next morning I packed my backpack and put my suggestion idea between the pages of my social studies book.

Kiran slumped out of his room as I made my way down the stairs. He didn't even bother to grunt at me or pull my hair. Daddy stood in front of the stove and banged a spoon against the side of a pot and muttered to himself. He reached for a towel and knocked over his tea. His cup only had a few sips left, but he still grumbled.

This wouldn't be a good time to tell him I'd rather make my own sandwich today instead of bringing the tiffin. Plus, Pride was a vice. I couldn't let what everyone else said bother me.

The onions Daddy had started to chop stung my

eyes as I reached over him for a bowl and cereal.

"Do you need some help?" I asked. Score! One karma point for being helpful. Only a billion more to go. At least I had a chance to practice all of this on Daddy, because the real test would be once I got to school and had to pretend I had no Anger when I was face-to-face with Lacy.

Daddy looked up. The lines on his face smoothed slightly, so that there were more pillow imprints than the hard creases the lines had been the second before.

"Thanks, *beta*. Just about finished. Making sardine masala."

"Daddy, there's a talk at the temple on the twenty-third. Do you think we can go?"

Daddy turned down the heat on the stove and looked at me. "A talk at the gurdwara?"

I nodded and poured milk into my cereal.

"I don't see why not. That'd be nice. It's a date." Daddy pushed my hair behind my ear. "Your dadima wouldn't want you to go to school with your hair loose."

Dadima only left her hair down after she'd washed it. Once it dried, she'd tie it back into a low bun. I'd left mine down today, hoping I could use it like a curtain to shield my face if I needed to.

Mom came into the kitchen dressed for work, her hair still wet from her shower.

"Morning," she said, grabbing a cup of coffee. "You're up early, darling. Meeting Sara?"

I shoved a huge spoonful of cereal into my mouth, making milk dribble down my chin. *Satnam Waheguru. Satnam Waheguru. Don't think bad thoughts, don't think bad thoughts.* Minus karma points for Anger at Mom's cluelessness, and probably Pride because it stung, and maybe even Attachment to Things of This World, even though Sara wasn't a "thing." I was really attached to the idea of our friendship, and I still couldn't let it go. Who knew all of this stuff could be so mixed together? At this rate I'd be sporting a mustache the rest of my life and probably grow a beard on top of it all.

"How about chicken pesto bake tonight?" Mom asked.

I shrugged.

"I'll be home at five and ready to cook," she said, and kissed Daddy on the way out the door.

Daddy handed me my tiffin. It was too hot to put into my backpack, so I had to carry it in a reusable grocery bag. Taking a deep breath, I reminded myself that it was Pride to be worried about what other people thought.

As I walked into school, several girls stood around Lacy's locker, including Sara. She almost blended in with them, but the way she pulled at the sides of her skirt and kept checking the straps of her top made her stand out, and not in a good way. Lacy stood out in the good way that teachers, parents, and boys noticed.

David stood in front of his locker, struggling with his waist pack. Lacy stuck her front teeth out over her bottom lip and mimicked a mouse. The other girls laughed at her impression of David. I couldn't believe Sara, Kate, and Emma would actually laugh at Lacy's stupid idea of a joke and not tell her David was off-limits.

Lacy looked up at me.

"Brought Curry Hut for lunch again, Kar?" she said.

I turned and stared hard at my lock. I had to squint my eyes in concentration. The numbers blurred together, so I had to blink a few times. That must have been a couple of extra karma points for ignoring Lacy.

Lacy turned back to the group of girls. "That's

why I don't dare eat at the Indian Garden. It'll put hair on your chest—or your face!"

Only the idea that Lacy would get her own slice of karma kept me from crying. I stood in front of my locker until their giggles mixed with the chatter and sounds coming from other classrooms and were nothing more than noise.

The rest of the morning I tried to melt into my desk. It was easy in Ms. Hillary's class, because all we did was a bunch of worksheets. But Mrs. Davis put us into groups in science to complete a chart about plant cells. Then in Mr. McKanna's class we did math relay races.

I'm good at math, so my row was actually excited to have me, despite my being 'Stache Attack. Lacy got all her problems wrong. Kate looked annoyed but laughed anyway.

It felt good to win and be better than Lacy at something, until I realized that Pride had crept in. Whatever karma points I'd earned this morning were getting deleted faster than I could earn more.

"Next time I want to be on your team, 'Stache," Derek said, putting his finger over his lip as he walked past my desk.

The whole 'Stache Attack thing confused me. It

was almost like he said "'Stache" in a good way, but why did it still make my breath catch in my chest like it was caught in a bubble? Insults should come with a usage guide like the grammar guide Ms. Hillary had in English class.

"If I ever want to know how to look like an idiot, I'll be sure to ask Derek," Ginny said, stopping at my desk.

I shrugged, not sure if I could open my mouth to laugh or say anything.

"Seriously, just ignore him. Come on." She pulled jokingly on my arm.

I fell in step beside Ginny, surprised and also relieved at how easy it was to be next to her.

"Did you come up with an idea for the suggestion box?" Ginny asked.

"Yeah. I did. I hope—" I stopped myself from saying I hoped it'd help clean up my karma. Ginny was really nice, but we were still only school friends. I didn't know if I could tell her more just yet. "I hope I can do something, you know, to help others."

"I love your idea about bringing a bag lunch, but I really want to start a recycling club. You should see the playground on Sundays. It's gross."

"You come to school on Sundays?"

Ginny blushed. "Not to school, but . . ." She glanced over her shoulder. No one noticed us. They were busy talking and laughing with each other. "Are you free after school?"

"Um. Yeah. I guess."

"Okay. After school I'll show you."

"Okay." I could tell by how she'd looked over her shoulder that she probably hadn't told anyone else about whatever it was.

"So what's your idea for the suggestion box?" Ginny asked.

"I was thinking a study group would be a good idea."

"Really? Like peer tutoring?" Ginny asked.

"Yeah. Exactly." I loved that Ginny actually listened to what I said and asked questions about it. Sara had always been good with listening and advice—before.

We filed into Mrs. Clark's class for social studies.

"How did your brainstorming go yesterday? Did all of you come up with a big idea?" Mrs. Clark asked once most of the class had settled down.

"Today?" Tom asked. "I thought you said Friday."

"I said today, and each of you should consider

putting your ideas in the suggestion box before you head off to lunch."

After class I put my study group idea in the suggestion box. Ginny had her recycling club idea ready too. She pushed it in and smiled at me. Maybe my karma was already getting better.

Ginny even waited as I got my tiffin out of the storage closet, and we walked to the lunchroom together. David smiled as we sat across from him at the table. The white bread from his sandwich clung to his teeth, forming little balls. It was really gross, but I smiled back anyway.

David had small containers with candy inside, and the bigger containers had egg salad in one and green Jell-O in another. White bread and candy were the last things I thought anyone with David's orthodontic problems should be eating.

It looked like Ruthie had packed his lunch for him.

David noticed me staring and started to say something, but more white bread stuck to the roof of his mouth. He had to stick his finger in and take out his retainer and scrape the bread off.

I rested my hands on top of the tiffin, considering whether or not I should open it. I looked down the table to make sure Lacy wasn't watching. I caught Sara's eye for half a breath. She turned her attention back to her school lunch and poked at the peas with her fork. Sara hated peas. That's something a best friend knows. I didn't know if Lacy knew that, or if she even cared.

"You can have half my sandwich if you want." Ginny held half of her sandwich out to me.

"Really?"

Ginny shrugged. "Sure."

"Hey," David said, and coughed. Some of his spit landed on the sandwich in Ginny's hand. "You always give it to Scoo—I mean . . . me."

David glared at me, the fluorescent lights reflecting off his glasses in an eerie way.

"It's okay," I said. "I should actually eat this, or my dad will get really annoyed. He just made it this morning."

"All right," Ginny said, and tossed the sandwich half to David.

I didn't know why David wanted the sandwich so badly when he had his own lunch. Then I watched him shove it into his pee pack. I sat up straighter, not sure what had just happened.

Ginny started to laugh, but not one of those

giggles where she covered her mouth, like most girls. It was a deep, choppy helicopter of a laugh. It made me smile and want to be her friend even more.

"Did he just—? I mean . . . isn't that—?"

"It's not what you think," Ginny said, still laughing.

Ginny's laugh filled up my arms and legs with a carefree lightness that I hadn't felt in several days. I reached for my tiffin and pulled off the lid, too full of that breezy I've-just-made-a-new-friend feeling to care if anyone noticed the smell of my lunch.

I had about three bites of sardine masala with about half a chapati before Tom said anything.

"Man, what is that, 'Stache Attack? Cat-food curry?"

Derek laughed, and they gave each other a high five.

"Can't you pack anything normal?" Lacy said, butting in.

"Something less 'Stache," Tom added while he chewed a huge bite of hot dog.

I wanted to say that in some countries roasted cockroaches on a stick would be considered normal and a hot dog would be strange, but I didn't have Ginny's ability to make words come out of my mouth with the same strength they had in my head.

"I know what my suggestion is going to be for the box," Lacy said, talking to the boys but loud enough to be heard at my table. "A smell-free lunch." She spread her hands apart as she said it like she could see the words written in the air.

I slipped the chapati bowl back on top of the sardine masala and ate the flat bread plain. The edges were hard without the sardine masala to moisten them, but the chewing gave me something to do. Ginny and David were silent, following the unspoken rule that after an onslaught of insults you had to remain quiet for a minimum of two or three minutes, out of respect.

Finally Ginny cleared her throat. "What's 'Stache'?"

"It's because Karma has hair on her face. Right above her lip. Like a mustache," David said, opening up his sandwich and picking out the olives.

I felt the chapati stick in my chest. I drank from my water bottle, but the feeling didn't go away.

"So what?" Ginny said. "Big deal."

Even though I'd waited all summer to hear those words from Sara, they didn't wash over me in the way I'd thought they would. It was nice of Ginny to say it, but someone else thinking my mustache wasn't a big deal didn't suddenly change the way I felt.

"Do you like your food?" Ginny asked, turning toward me.

I did, but I didn't know if I should admit it. Probably if things with Sara hadn't been so weird this summer, I'd have just said yes. But look where being myself had gotten me with her. Then again, Ginny didn't give me that nervous choose-the-right-door—one is a million dollars, the other is eternal doom—feeling I got with Sara.

"Yeah. Most of the time."

"I know someone who will eat it if you're not going to," David said, gathering up all his little plastic containers and shoving them back into his lunch box.

I had a mental image of David with sardine stuck between his teeth and little curry spittle sprayed across the table. "It's okay. I'll just eat it later at home."

"If you like it, you should eat it now," Ginny said.

"I guess." I couldn't help but look over at Sara and imagine what she'd tell me to do—if we were still friends, that is. But she had her back to me.

Ginny had a point, but each time I heard some-one laugh or sniff, I wanted to find a closet to hide in because I was positive it had to do with 'Stache Attack or my tiffin.

Earning karma points and trying to pretend the teasing didn't bother me wasn't going to be sprinkle-of-fairy-dust easy.

Chapter Eighteen

Ginny waited for me at my desk after school, and we just kind of fell into step with each other. A purposeful wait and walk.

"Follow me," she said. We walked out the gate toward our houses, but Ginny grabbed my arm and we turned left.

"Are we going to the elementary school?" I asked, keeping my voice low so the crossing guard wouldn't hear.

"Yeah," Ginny whispered. "Don't worry. No one will be there, and we're going to the playground by the kindergarten anyway. It's always the first to be empty."

My heart flip-flopped like a fish on dry ground. I was pretty sure we were breaking a couple of rules, maybe even trespassing, which couldn't be good for my karma point count.

"This way," Ginny said when we got to the tree line at the side of the kindergarten buildings. "We have to go behind the tool shed, then up onto the climbing frame."

My breath caught in my throat. I had an image of the principal's scowling face hovering over us.

"Don't worry. No one will be able to see us," Ginny said, reading my thoughts.

I followed her onto the climbing frame and up to a platform about the size of my bed.

"Well?" Ginny asked.

I looked around. Three sides of the platform were solid and decorated to be like a ship. The fourth side opened to three steps leading up to the rest of the climbing frame. A large solid wall for rock climbing blocked us from being seen by anyone in the school buildings—the perfect place to be alone or with a good friend. The idea that we might actually be more than school friends surprised me. I did consider Ginny my real friend.

"It's great," I said.

"Right?" Ginny leaned back against a side of the climbing frame, with a steering wheel above her head.

"I love coming here to read and draw or just think."

I nodded, picturing myself doing all those things in exactly this spot.

"The only thing is, a bunch of older kids come here on Saturday nights and trash it. So on Sunday morning I usually pick the garbage up. I just can't concentrate until it's all clean. That's why I want to put more trash cans and recycling bins around the school."

"Your mom lets you come here alone on the weekend?" I asked.

"I don't really tell her. My baby brother is only a couple of months old. She usually falls asleep when he's napping. Then I come out here to enjoy being free."

"You could always come over to my house," I said. I hadn't really thought first before saying it, and my cheeks flushed after I did.

"That'd be cool. Thanks."

I pulled out my tiffin. "Want to help me eat my sardine masala?"

"Sure." Ginny took the bread I handed her, and I showed her how to tear and roll it before dipping it into the masala. "It's actually pretty good. It doesn't taste at all like I thought it would."

We finished the rest of the masala before Ginny asked, "Can I ask you something?"

"Sure."

"When did they start with the 'Stache Attack thing?"

Even though Ginny didn't say "'Stache Attack" in a teasing way, it stung just the same.

"It started at the pool." I swallowed a bite and felt it slide down my throat. Then I explained about Lacy and the snack bar that day. Ginny nodded as I described how Sara didn't do or say anything as everyone laughed. My throat squeezed together when I said Sara's name, but the words kept coming. The more I talked about it, the closer I felt to Ginny, which was funny, because talking about my mustache had been what had made me feel even further away from Sara.

"That sucks," Ginny said. She chewed the last bite of chapati. "Do you remember in first grade when Derek called me 'Guinea Pig' for the first time?"

I scratched the tips of my ears where they burned. Talking about 'Stache Attack embarrassed me enough, but for some reason it embarrassed me more to listen to Ginny talk about her nickname.

"Well, do you know that the entire summer before that, Derek and I played together? Every day?" Ginny stared up at the sky as she talked. "His grandma lives next door to me, and she used to watch him while his mom went to work."

She took a deep breath. I sat quietly, not wanting to break the spell that spread between us, solidifying our friendship, making Ginny want to spill her secrets.

"We even took baths together."

"Baths?"

Our eyes met, and we cracked up, not in a spell-breaking way. In fact, it made the spell swell and engulf all our fears and hesitations, and pop them like bubbles.

"I know. My mom took our picture once and gave a copy to his grandma," Ginny said, shaking her head. "But then in first grade, when he accidentally pronounced my name as 'guinea,' well, he was too embarrassed to admit that it was an accident. He liked that everyone thought he was funny, and he pretended he'd done it on purpose. It was better to be funny than be best friends with Guinea Pig."

"Didn't you care that he made it such a big joke?"

"I thought it would all die down and we'd still

play together after school. But he made lots of new friends, especially with the other boys. So I guess I knew it was over."

Neither of us said anything for a few seconds.

"I did care for a while," Ginny said. "Sometimes I still do."

"I'm sorry I never said anything when people called you 'Guinea Pig.'"

The memory of Sara looking away at the pool was still as vivid as the day it happened. I could see it like my brain had taken a photo of it and was displaying it behind my eyes. I wondered how many of those kinds of moments were still snapshots in Ginny's head. Until Sara had sat quietly around this past week, I never really got it that sometimes the silence hurts worse than the teasing.

Chapter Nineteen

The next day I thought about dumping the prawn sambal down the drain that ran alongside the road. Standing at the top of the hill, I looked back toward my house. Daddy couldn't see me. It would be quick. A simple flip of the wrist.

Two things stopped me. One, the fact that prawns were expensive, and Daddy made it very clear just how much each prawn cost and just how many hours of work it took to make that kind of money. Daddy freaked out about money the way I freaked out about diseases, maybe even more so now, with Mom the only one working.

The other thing stopping me was that I wanted to be strong enough to ignore Derek and Lacy when they made fun of my lunch. I wanted to get rid of that burn in my chest when they said stupid things. No more Pride. No more Anger. It didn't seem possible to keep tally of my karma points, because just when I thought I'd earned some, I'd lose more than I'd earned.

At school, in math, Mr. McKanna paired us up and passed out Math Scrabble games. Then he stopped at my desk and in front of everyone said, "Karma, can you please stay after class? I need to discuss something with you."

I avoided everyone's eyes and nodded. Teachers don't normally single me out unless I've raised my hand. It took extra concentration to gather my tiles and line them up nicely on the holder.

Math Scrabble was basically regular Scrabble but with numbers and addition, subtraction, division, and multiplication signs. It's played in rounds. The winner moves to the next table, and eventually the top two winners go head-to-head in the champion-ship ring, as Mr. McKanna called it, but the cham-pionship ring was just two desks pushed together in the middle of the room.

I didn't want to win, because I didn't want the added attention, but my thoughts were so preoccu-pied trying to keep my mind off what Mr. McKanna could possibly need to discuss with me that I kept winning. Five minutes before the bell, I sat in the championship ring facing Kate.

"Come on, Kate!" Lacy said, nudging the other girls to join.

"Yeah, Kate."

"You can do it, Kate."

I looked across the desk as Kate busied herself, placing her tiles neatly on the holder. Her eyes met mine, and I smiled. Kate smiled back, but Lacy cleared her throat. Kate's mouth slid back into a straight line.

"You got it, Karma," Ginny said.

I nodded at her gratefully.

"Yeah, Karma," David chimed in.

Tom leaned forward and pretended to scratch the bottom of his nose, but uncurled his finger in a 'Stache Attack. "Sneaky 'Stache!"

"All right! All right!" Mr. McKanna stepped forward, hushing the giggles.

I stared down at my tiles, trying to focus on the game. Kate placed a simple addition number equation on the board, and the game had begun. When I gathered my tiles, Tom rubbed his upper lip in that stupid Sneaky 'Stache way. It made me think. I knew what Mr. McKanna wanted to discuss.

My mustache.

How long had the teachers been discussing it? They'd probably noticed and wanted Mr. McKanna to discuss shaving tips with me.

A couple of minutes later I held the winning tile in my hand, but it gave me no satisfaction when I placed it down and won.

"That's what I call a close *shave*, Karma!" Derek said.

"Totally! It was getting pretty *hairy* there for a while," Tom added.

They both put their finger over their upper lip and said, "You've been 'Stached!" right in Kate's face.

"Ugh," Kate sighed, pushing them away.

The bell rang, and I hoped Mr. McKanna had forgotten that he wanted to talk to me, so I could slip out of the room and disappear into the hallway.

"Oh, Kar," Lacy said too loudly. "Doesn't Mr. McKanna want to discuss something with you?"

Lacy smiled in a way that reminded me of cotton candy, like that one time when I went to a baseball game with Daddy. I ate three bags because he only had a twenty-dollar bill, and the guy walking up and down the aisles selling cotton candy didn't have change. My stomach ached the entire night and I'd never wanted cotton candy since. Lacy's cotton candy smile was sweet, sticky, and fluffy, and it made me sick to my stomach.

I grabbed my books and held them close to my chest as I stared at the floor, waiting for everyone else to leave the classroom.

"Have a seat, Karma," Mr. McKanna said once everyone had filed out of the room.

I noticed the black hair on his arms and how it extended all the way to the tops of his hands and then into little tufts on his fingers. I rubbed my arms, and while I knew they were hairy, it made me glad they weren't *that* hairy. Yet Kiran once told me that hair, noses, and ears never stopped growing. Would my arms be as hairy as Mr. McKanna's when I was an adult?

Maybe when he was a kid, a teacher also talked to him about his hair. I bet that's what all the teachers talked about at lunchtime.

"Are you okay?" Mr. McKanna asked. "You look kind of pale and scared."

I shook my head, but then realized it might mean I wasn't okay, so I nodded. Then again, nodding might make him think I was scared. I had to say something. "It's not hairy—I mean scary. I'm just—"

Mr. McKanna laughed and rubbed his arms. I must have still been staring at them. "It's okay. You're not in trouble, Karma." He cleared his throat and ran his hand over his mouth and chin.

So, this *was* about my mustache. He'd just touched his mouth. Wasn't that something police watched for when they asked criminals questions? They watched what criminals did with their hands and eyes.

I felt my own hand itch to touch my upper lip, but I fought the urge. I didn't want to be obvious, so I pretended to scratch the bottom of my nose, but that looked like I picked my nose, so I turned my finger and rubbed the bottom of my nose with the side of my finger.

Mr. McKanna gave me a funny look and rubbed the bottom of his nose the same way, like maybe I was telling him he had something hanging off the end of his nose. I shoved my hands under my legs and waited for him to tell me the best way to get a clean, close shave, wishing that my karma was as sparkly as Lacy's shoes.

"So, anyway," he continued, "Lacy's mom called yesterday. I'd wanted to talk to you before, and her calling was like an omen, you know?" He smiled.

I didn't know what could be so funny about an omen to talk to an eleven-year-old girl about facial hair.

"The thing is, a particularly interesting suggestion in the box from your homeroom caught my attention, and the teachers are pretty excited about it. We'd like to start a peer study group. Mrs. Clark suggested we call it Study Buddies. I called your dad and he's on board, but I wanted to know how you felt about helping Lacy out with her math." He paused and watched me.

It took a few seconds for it all to sink in. Lacy needed help with math. Mr. McKanna didn't say anything about shaving.

"For now it'll just be informal tutoring. Mrs. Jenkins asked if you'd be free Tuesdays and Thursdays after school. Once we have approval from the school board, we'll give you and some of the other students, perhaps Kate and Sara and a few others, an office in the study hall. Kids can come and visit you when they need help with their homework or studying for a test. Of course, the school board will want to see results before they put money into study materials, but that's our goal. Would you be interested in getting involved?"

I nodded to keep the room from spinning. Anything was better than having to discuss my mustache with a teacher, even if it meant I'd have to help Lacy with her math homework.

Chapter Twenty

When I walked into the kitchen after school, Daddy held a plate of vegetable pakoras in his hands and smiled so big, I thought tears would squeeze out of his eyes.

"Ah, my little professor!" Of course Daddy would make a big deal about the tutoring thing.

I grabbed a pakora and pretended I didn't notice Daddy's misty eyes. Since Mom had started working, all I'd wanted was for someone to notice me, but now that Daddy was staring at me with a goofy grin and frying up my favorite snack, I wanted it to stop. I didn't really deserve the attention. Tutoring Lacy wasn't really my idea. I'd thought Study Buddies would mean tutoring kids over at the elementary school, not my arch-nemesis.

The more time I'd had to consider Mr. McKanna's idea, the less I thought of it as a good one. Lacy wouldn't be happy about getting help from me, and there wasn't even a small chance she'd make it pleasant for me, I could be sure of that.

I finished the pakora quickly while standing, even though Daddy had just taken it out of the fryer. It burned my mouth so badly, I couldn't really taste it.

"I've got a lot of homework," I said, leaning sideways, like my bag was weighing me down.

Daddy quickly wrapped two more pakoras in a napkin. "Go, go, go. I'll get you when dinner is ready." He shoved me toward the steps and sniffed.

I didn't actually have much homework, so I pulled the tiffin out of my bag and sat on my bed, eating the pakoras and the prawn sambal I never ate at lunch. The prawns were room temperature, but my stomach had been growling since last period, and I didn't want to send any accidental message to Babaji that I didn't need his blessings. Because I did. I needed all the blessings I could get.

When I'd finished eating, I sat back on my bed. The last two days after school, I'd been so busy cooking and cleaning, I hadn't noticed how much time stretched between school and dinner. But today Daddy had cleaned the entire house and had dinner under control. I only had a few pages to read in English and a science worksheet on genes to complete, but I didn't want to start it now.

Out of habit I reached for the phone. My finger found the nine, ready to push the rest of Sara's number. I couldn't even remember how all of our conversations used to start. How did the simple routine of calling your best friend go from being something you did every day without thinking to something you sat on your bed worrying about?

My palms were slick and I wiped them on my shorts after I hung up the phone. I could imagine exactly where Sara would be standing if I called. I could picture Ruthie grabbing for the phone and pulling on Sara's shirt. I didn't know how much longer I'd be able to picture it all accurately.

Dadima had been the same. I used to see her out of the corner of my eye the weeks just after she died. I'd catch a shadow of her shape in the kitchen or on her bed saying prayers. Her voice would whisper little reminders to me or I'd be alone and the pressure of her hands on my shoulders or a tap on my back would startle me. Then, one day, it stopped. I couldn't remember how her voice sounded. I couldn't smell her. I stopped seeing her. She had disappeared. I had to close my eyes really tight to remember how her earlobes had drooped and how the hair around her face had been white and coarse, or the wideness of her hands, or how young she'd looked when she closed her eyes while she recited from her prayer book.

Little by little Sara had started disappearing. After days of her being attached to Lacy's side and not standing up for me, our friendship had started to die too.

Dadima once explained that everything must die in order for something new to grow.

"Imagine each of our souls is a drop of water and God is the ocean. We are separated from God until we find the ocean and become one with God. The drop of water isn't gone. It's simply in a new form. *Marnae hee tae paeeaae pooran parmaanand.*"

That meant "In death alone is one blessed with supreme bliss."

"Are you afraid to die?" I'd asked, suddenly aware how easily she spoke of death and how much I didn't want to lose her.

"Why would I fear supreme bliss?"

I hardly considered the death of Sara's friendship supreme bliss. It turned out to be more of a karma catastrophe. And just so karma could really rub it in, it had paired me with Lacy.

Both Kiran and Mom were already seated at the table when Daddy called me down for dinner. Takeout boxes from Supremo's were lined up in the middle of the table.

"What's all this for?" I asked, trying to sound cheerful. Normally this was my favorite dinner, but since the throw-up incident there, I hadn't really been in the mood for pizza. My cheeks flushed at the memory, but I pushed it aside, along with the pinprick of annoyance I felt that my parents were so clueless about everything.

"For you. What an achievement!" Mom stood up and hugged me.

Daddy whistled as he scooped some salad and pizza onto a plate for me. Even Kiran didn't have a scowl on his face. He wasn't exactly smiling either, but it was an improvement.

Looking at my family right then was like rewinding our lives to three months ago—everyone around the table, no stress lines or forced smiles. I didn't want to ruin the moment, so I even ignored Daddy when he poured hot sauce all over his pizza and salad.

"I'm very proud of you, Karmajeet." Daddy said. "You have a gift, and I'm glad you're putting it to use." He cleared his throat as he set the bottle of hot sauce down and glanced at Kiran.

Kiran stared into his glass of water.

"Daddy said that Mr. McKanna mentioned that this was just a trial, before they officially get Study Buddies started," Mom said. "How come he wants you to do this now?"

"Oh, there's a new girl in my class and her mom wants her to get some extra help." I took a bite of salad, making sure I got dressing, a tomato, cheese, and a crouton all in the same bite.

"Oh, is it that girl Sara's mom mentioned? She just moved across the street from them," Mom said.

"Yep," I said, glad that my mouth was full so I didn't have to elaborate.

"That's nice. Maybe the two of you could become friends." Mom smiled. "You and Sara need to make some more friends in middle school. It's your chance to branch out. Right, Kiran?"

Kiran kept his eyes on his water. Mom reached

across the table and patted him on the hand gently.

"Sure," he mumbled, forcing a bite of pizza into his mouth.

Daddy dropped his fork with a clatter, and it sent a piece of lettuce drizzled in hot sauce flying into the middle of the table.

"Listen here, young man," Daddy said. "I didn't raise a bunch of Neanderthals." He pushed up from his chair so that he towered over Kiran. "I expect you to speak actual words, not mumble responses when your mother asks you a question."

Daddy breathed through his nose, his mouth hidden under his mustache. It was a serious moment, but I could only focus on Daddy's mustache hair going in and out of his nose as he breathed. I didn't know how he didn't sneeze.

"Fine." Kiran pushed away from the table and stood up too. He stood at almost the same height as Daddy. He turned to me. "Yes, Karma. Junior high and high school are really great. You get to make all kinds of super friends and have wonderful experiences. It's real swell when kids twice your size find it funny to screw up your chemistry experiment and then send you to the smoker's bathroom as a prank so your own teachers and parents think you're a complete loser." His voice sounded the same as a man reading a toothpaste commercial. He turned and looked directly at Daddy. "That what you want?"

Kiran tossed his plate and cup into the sink and ran upstairs. Daddy plopped back down into his seat. We were still sitting in silence when he started to play his guitar with the amp on full volume.

Daddy pointed at Mom with his fork. "This is because of you."

"Oh, come on. We both agreed guitar was a suitable instrument. We have to give them small choices." She stared down at her plate and shook her head.

"It's not just the guitar. It's everything. He's purposely doing poorly in his advanced classes, and he's in with a bad group." Daddy pushed his plate away. "This is a result of the last five years of you letting him have it easy. You didn't push him enough."

"Maybe this has more to do with you pushing too hard." Mom stood up and took her plate to the sink.

Daddy closed himself in his study, and Mom went upstairs. I sat alone at the table, knowing I'd have to clean up my celebration dinner. Somehow, I didn't think I'd ever eat Supremo's again.

As I washed the dishes, I couldn't help but think my karma had plummeted so low that it now affected my entire family.

Chapter Twenty-One

Lacy's mom had been eager to get Study Buddies started but had made it very clear that no one was to find out that Lacy was getting extra help. She called Mr. McKanna, who then explained to me that tutoring Lacy at school would lower Lacy's self-confidence, which was already lacking in math. I nodded like I agreed, but I knew the only thing Lacy lacked was the ability to be nice.

As we were packing our bags at the end of the day, Ginny said bye and headed over to Mrs. Clark's room. "I hope she wants to talk about the recycling club."

"But it's anonymous."

"Like anyone else has recycling magnets all over their locker or wears shirts like this." She pulled her T-shirt at the bottom to make her point. It was a girl hugging a tree and the tree branches hugging her back.

"True. Well, my fingers are crossed for you."

Right after she left, Mr. McKanna knocked on the classroom door. "May I speak to Karma, please?"

Derek tittered and gave the third 'Stache Attack of the day as I walked toward the classroom door.

"I'm glad I caught you," Mr. McKanna said, handing me a folder. "I've put a few worksheets and Lacy's last quiz in here so you can review the mistakes with her. Also, we have a test coming up in two weeks and I included a study sheet for that. Have fun." He turned and walked back to his classroom.

Have fun tutoring *Lacy*?

I took a deep breath and whispered, *"Satnam Waheguru."* Putting up with Lacy might just be the karma boost I needed to push me out of my current slump, but I still wasn't looking forward to it and definitely didn't expect to have fun.

At the bus bell, I tried to get lost in the mass of kids pouring out the door. It was a relief not to have to lie to Ginny about why I was taking the bus or where I was going.

When I climbed onto the bus, Sara and Lacy were already there, sitting next to each other behind Ruthie. Sara didn't seem at all surprised to see me on her bus. She kept her eyes glued to the magazine Lacy had splayed over their laps. Lacy barely looked over at me as I got to the top step. She leaned closer to Sara and whispered something. I had no idea what she'd told Sara about what I was doing there, or how she'd explain me following her into her house later when we got off the bus.

"Karma!" Ruthie called when she saw me.

I waved, wanting so badly to slide into the seat next to her, but a girl her age already sat there.

"Are you coming over to play?" Ruthie asked.

Some older girls across the aisle snickered, their eyes targeting me.

"Not today, Ruthie." I quickly shoved further down the aisle and out of the target zone. I slid into a seat too close to the back of the bus for my liking.

The boy next to me took up over half the seat and was asleep or doing a good job pretending to be. I readjusted my bag several times. I didn't know if I should put it on my lap, between my knees, or on the floor on top of my shoes. Then there was the matter of either slumping forward or sitting with my back flat against the straight-backed bench. Nothing I did felt normal on the green, plastic seats. The few times I'd ridden home with Sara in the past, we'd sat near the front, and I'd never noticed the dead bugs dried in the windowsills or the weird black blobs of gunk that patterned the floor.

I clutched my bag to my chest. I kept my face buried in it, partly to avoid eye contact with anyone and partly so I could inhale my own germs. What felt like an hour later, the bus made familiar turns closer to Sara and Lacy's neighborhood.

I took a deep breath and whispered, *"Satnam Waheguru."*

By the time I got to the bottom of the bus steps, Sara already had Ruthie by the hand, rushing her across the street. I mean, the bus driver *was* waving them on, and the flashing lights couldn't wait for us to make up and decide to be best friends again.

My body and brain tugged me in opposite directions. I wanted to run up to Sara and cross the street with her and Ruthie, to go inside their house, have a snack, and hang out in her basement like nothing was weird between us. But she had hurried Ruthie across the street without looking back at me.

Lacy's front door opened as I jogged after her across the front yard. A mom-type lady with blondish-gray hair stood in the doorway. And, just as I'd imagined, she wore an apron and a smear of flour across her left cheek.

Lacy ducked under her mom's arm. For about half a second her mom's happy expression sagged like she'd expected a hug. Mrs. Jenkins quickly brightened when she looked at me, and she grabbed my right hand with both of hers.

"Oh, how nice to meet you, Karma! I'm just so glad you are able to help Lacy. Come in, come in."

Mrs. Jenkins led me inside to a sparsely decorated room with several boxes stacked along a wall. A couch sat alone in the middle of the room, and the air smelled like fresh paint.

"I've spent two hours trying to get some goodies ready so you girls can snack and study." Lacy's mom lifted a plate toward us.

"Mom, what is *that*?" Lacy asked, scrunching her nose.

Mrs. Jenkins pushed out a laugh and waved her hand in the air. "I know. I know. Cooking is not really my thing, but Karma's our first guest, and I wanted to do something special."

The plate was stacked with fruit and marsh-mallows stuck on long sticks.

"Fruit kebabs! I got the idea from a magazine." Mrs. Jenkins looked extremely pleased with her creations.

I reached for a stick to be polite.

Mrs. Jenkins gently set the plate down on the counter and watched with an expectant smile as I took a bite.

"Thanks," I said, nodding and chewing. "It's nice."

"Oh, you're too sweet."

"We've got a lot of work to do," Lacy said, throwing her backpack onto a chair at the dining table in the middle of the kitchen.

"Of course, of course." A timer buzzed, and Mrs. Jenkins reached for a hand towel and ran to the oven. "Cookies. I almost forgot."

She pulled out a cookie sheet full of flat, crispy discs.

Lacy slouched into a chair at the dining table with a sigh.

"Those look good, Mrs. Jenkins," I said, even though it looked like she'd forgotten an ingredient or two.

"Thank you, Karma. But please don't call me that dreadful name. I'm a Miss now anyways. I'd rather you call me Rose."

"Umm. Okay." I finished the fruit-and-marshmallow kebab and hoped Lacy would butt in and say something soon. Lacy's mom was nice, but it made me uncomfortable how much she talked. Plus, Daddy never let me call an adult by their first name. I really hoped she wouldn't force me to call her Rose.

"Well, I'll just leave these here to cool." Lacy's mom put the tray on the counter. "Oh, and I called your father, Karma, to let him know I have a job interview. So he'll be here at five to get you." She turned to Lacy. "I'll be back by dinner. If it's any later, I'll call you." She moved to leave, but then turned around. "Just in case, there are frozen dinners and make sure you have a glass of milk—"

"Mom!"

"Okay. Okay." She tried to give Lacy a kiss on the cheek before turning to me. "Oh, things have just been so crazy these past few weeks. You know, moving here and then trying to find a job." She sighed and pushed her hair off her face. "I'm sure that's why Lacy's behind in math. I mean, I used to blame her father—"

"Mom."

"I know. I'll be late. You girls help yourselves to the snacks. I'm just so scattered, you know? But I told Lacy this move would be the best thing for us. A new start, right?"

I nodded and smiled as she continued to talk, even though I was having a hard time following her.

"I just thought holding Lacy back a year would be best—"

Lacy stood up and pushed her mom's purse into her arms. "Bye."

Mrs. Jenkins hugged the bag with one arm and threw the other up in surrender. "All right, I'm going." She waved and stepped out the front door.

Lacy stared down at the flat, burned cookies and the marshmallows and fruit stuck on sticks. I had a pretty good idea how she felt, probably the same as one of the strawberries stabbed by a wooden stick.

We stood there in silence.

"She's crazy, okay? Nothing she said is true. Let's just do our work."

I opened up my math book and dug around in my school bag for two pencils and some paper. I wanted to pretend that I hadn't just heard Lacy's mom say that Lacy had been held back, but my gut pinched together, nudging me to say something nice. And not just for karma's sake.

"You know, things are pretty crazy at my house too," I said, staring at the dining table. As I said it, Daddy's scowl, Mom's rushing and stress, and Kiran's angry guitar strumming all flashed through my mind, warming my ears.

"Just tell me how to do this algebra stuff, okay? I don't want to talk about anything, and I don't have anything to talk about."

Looking at Lacy sitting at her dining table without her fan club in tow, she looked less like Lacy and more like a normal girl. I almost felt sorry for her.

Chapter Twenty-Two

Sweat sprinkled my upper lip the next morning as Lacy stared at me from Sara's locker. I knew she was worried I'd tell what I'd found out about her the day before, but I wouldn't. Not because the thought hadn't crossed my mind, but because I didn't want to disappoint Mr. McKanna.

"What's up with Goldi-looks-a-lot?" Ginny asked, nudging me with her elbow.

"What do you mean?" I cleared my throat and slammed my locker too hard.

Ginny laughed. "She keeps staring at you like she's afraid you'll, I don't know, disappear or something."

"Ha! Yeah, right. She'd probably love it if I disappeared." I tried to force out a laugh but sprayed my books with spit instead. I used my sleeve to wipe it off.

"Your hair looks nice today, Kar," Lacy said, walking past my locker, trailed by Sara. "Have you been using that avocado hair mask we talked about?"

Her words were like brownies right out of the oven. They smelled good, full of yummy promise, but really they'd burn my mouth if I dared take a bite.

Sara's mouth opened like she wanted to ask something, but she looked at me and closed her mouth, hurrying after Lacy into the classroom.

Ginny raised her eyebrow at me. "What's she talking about? An avocado mask?"

I shook my head and rolled my eyes.

I didn't want to know Lacy's stupid secret that she'd been held back. I didn't want to feel like everything I did and said was a big lie. Especially when it came to Ginny.

The only good thing about having Lacy stare at me all day was that I was pretty sure I had the upper hand. She didn't want me to spill her secret, so I didn't think she'd make fun of my lunch. Her words at the lockers were a subtle warning that gave my skin goose bumps, but as long as I didn't tell her secret, I could eat my lunch in peace.

"Hey, how come you didn't walk home yesterday?"

I fiddled with the clasp of my tiffin. "Oh, yeah. Yesterday. Mr. McKanna needed me to do something."

"Really? What?"

"Oh, just something about math."

"Duh, really? He is our math teacher." Ginny laughed but looked sideways at me as she tossed David a carrot stick.

I took a bite of my chicken curry but still couldn't help glancing toward Lacy as I did.

"Karma," Ginny said, "David and I need to tell you something."

Something in Ginny's voice snagged my attention. She clenched her jaw just the way Sara did when she wanted to say something to me but didn't really know how to say it. I held my breath and prepared to hear the worst.

This was it. I was officially going to be de-friended by Ginny and David. And just when I was beginning to get used to things. I poked the chicken with my fork and took a deep breath. Lots of oxygen. No palpitations.

"David, do you want to tell her?" Ginny asked.

David pulled a piece of lettuce out of his sandwich and shoved it into his mouth. He shook his head.

"Okay, then." Ginny put her carrot stick down and turned to face me.

I told myself to hold it together and not cry. I would just offer to help Mr. McKanna grade papers or ask the secretary if she needed help filing detentions during lunch. It was no big deal being de-friended, again.

Ginny glanced around and lowered her voice. "David doesn't carry his pee around in that waist pack." She stopped and stared at me.

Huh? Wait, were we still friends? She wanted to tell me about David's pee? At lunch? While I was supposed to be eating?

Where in the world did his pee go, then? I imagined tubes that went from the pee pack down into his socks, like the blue gel insoles Daddy used to wear when he lectured at the university. Instead of that gooey, blue filling, I pictured an amber yellow. I blinked and straightened my back. Gross.

Ginny raised her eyebrow and laughed. "Whatever you're thinking, it's not that bad. Let me explain." She cleared her throat and continued.

"He did need the pack last year, but over the summer they did another surgery. Now he can use the toilet just fine, but his sister got a new cat. David's afraid it'll eat his gerbil, Scooter. So he puts Scooter in the waist pack." Ginny paused to let me digest what she'd just said.

I started to laugh when I thought about all the times David got stuck in his desk, or how he put food into his waist pack or how often he put his hand protectively over it. He wasn't protecting medical equipment but a gerbil!

Ginny laughed too and shoved me in a joking way. I shoved her back and threw a piece of chapati at David.

He smiled his big, crowded-teeth grin back at me and shoved the chapati into the waist pack. That made me laugh even harder.

"Just don't tell anyone else about it, okay?" David said, suddenly getting serious.

"Don't tell anyone about what?"

Lacy's voice made me jump. My hand jerked back, and I had to grab for the tiffin, but it tipped, and the reddish-orange curry splattered down my leg. The warmth of the curry soaked through my jeans onto my skin.

Lacy stood behind David, glaring at me with razor-sharp eyes.

"Nothing. It's a secret," David said. His hand hovered near his waist pack.

Lacy's eyes bored into mine.

I shook my head in slow motion, watching Lacy's reaction carefully. I hoped she got the I-didn't-tell-your-secret vibe I shot her way.

She gave me one last squint before turning around and heading back to the lunch line. It was apple crumble day, and most people had brought extra money for one.

"You'd better rinse that before it sets," Ginny said. "I'll clean up the table."

"Thanks." I rushed to the bathroom. The stall door swung closed behind me as I fiddled with the toilet roll, trying to find the loose flap. I pulled off a big wad as the bathroom door swung open, letting in a roar of cafeteria voices. Footsteps clattered to the sinks and stopped. I recognized Sara's voice.

I reached carefully to click the stall door locked, so no one would find me bathed in curry. The toilet paper balled up on my jeans as I continued to rub at the mess. I really needed some water, but I couldn't go out there now.

"So what's the big secret?" It wasn't Lacy's voice. It was Kate.

"Yeah," Emma echoed. "All the crumble's going to be taken."

The smell of fake fruit wafted toward the stall.

"Swear you won't tell anyone?" Sara asked. Her voice didn't sound like the Sara I knew, definitely not the same girl who threatened to break her ruler over a boy's head in first grade when he asked me if I was adopted, after seeing my mom drop me off late to school. "Lacy was held back."

A collective gasp followed. I put my hand over my mouth. How did Sara know that?

"How do you know?" Kate asked.

"Yeah, she told me she's turning twelve on Friday," Emma added.

"It is her birthday, but she'll be thirteen. We did some Chinese zodiac thing in a magazine. You had to put your year of birth," Sara explained.

"No wonder her bra is a B cup," Emma said, all breathy.

"It does make sense," Kate added.

The bathroom door opened and they scattered. I flushed the toilet even though I hadn't done anything. I ducked out of the stall and splashed some water onto my jeans and dried them the best I could under the hand dryer.

Even if all summer Sara hadn't been herself, I still found it difficult to imagine her standing at the sinks, putting on lip gloss and spreading rumors. *And* rumors about Lacy.

That wasn't the Sara I knew. Maybe she wasn't really the Sara I wanted to know at all anymore.

During science I had to partner with Tom for a gene chart project—which was embarrassing on so many levels. Considering I had the dominant brown hair and brown eyes, four out of five times, any kids between Tom and me would end up looking just like me. If I ever became a teacher, I'd stick to plant gene projects.

Derek leaned across the aisle where he and Lacy sat, and pretended to read our chart. "Brown, brown, brown, brown, mustache," he said, putting his hand in a stupid 'Stache Attack.

I quickly pulled our chart away from him and stared at my name at the top of the paper, willing the letters to stay in focus and not get blurry.

"At least our kids will be smart," Tom said, raising his hand in a high five that no one reached for.

"Whatever. Our kids will be blond and totally cute." Lacy grabbed the paper from Derek and held it up like it was proof.

"They'll be blond, all right," Tom said with a laugh.

Lacy snapped her head back to Derek and then to Tom.

"What is that supposed to mean?" Lacy asked.

"Too dumb to figure it out? No wonder you were held back," Derek said. His goofy grin dropped as Lacy's face turned bright red.

Even though the conversation was happening right in front of my face, it felt like it was on television, and I could only watch, and not say anything to help.

"You're an idiot!" Lacy said at the same time the bell rang.

Derek and Tom laughed and bolted out the door.

Lacy turned to me. "What is it with you? Does your mustache make you spill people's secrets?"

"I didn't say anything!" My eyes burned and I bit down hard on my back teeth.

Lacy glared at me long and hard before she snatched up her gene chart and stomped away.

My nerves sizzled like butter dripping off chapati onto a hot pan. I guess I could have been happy that Lacy finally got her karma dished out to her. Instead it made my palms clammy and my stomach gurgle and knot up.

Lacy getting what she deserved didn't make me suddenly glow with a shiny newness or make any of my mustache hairs fall out. I'd double-checked before school. Still seventeen.

It was only when the bus bell rang, taking Lacy with it, that I managed to take a deep breath.

"You okay?" Ginny asked.

"Oh. Um. Yeah. Just got a lot of homework, that's all."

"You do?" She squinted her eyes.

I shrugged, pretty sure I'd just lied. Again.

"Hey, you want to help me make posters tomorrow? Mrs. Clark asked me to make posters for the new recycling club. I get to put them up in the lunchroom on Friday."

My excitement for Ginny let me forget Lacy for a minute. "That's great. I'd love to help. How about during lunch or something?"

"Actually, can we do it at your house? It's just that the art room is used during our lunch period and my baby brother is usually napping when I get home."

Tomorrow was Thursday. Thursday was secret Study Buddies with Lacy. She was supposed to walk home with me, and I still hadn't figured out how to explain to Ginny why Lacy was following me home.

"I really want to. It's just that I have this thing tomorrow that I totally forgot about." Was it a lie when you knew you said something mostly true but kind of not true?

"Oh. Okay, no big deal." Ginny shrugged.

But it was a big deal. Karma points aside, I'd just lied for about the tenth time to the only person who had been nice to me all year.

Chapter Twenty-Three

Daddy sang along to the Bollywood music blaring from his computer as he stirred the dal for my lunch on Friday morning before school.

"I'm really looking forward to the talk tonight, *beta*. You?"

"Mmm-hmm." I quickly shoved a bite of aloo paratha into my mouth. The spicy potato mixture coated my tongue like glue.

"It's so wonderful that you're taking the initiative to understand and learn about Sikhism. Your dadima would be so proud."

Would Dadima be proud?

I wasn't even sure why I'd thought the talk was such a good idea in the first place. Trying to clean up my karma had sounded so simple in the beginning, but I had nothing to show for it. Aside from Ginny and David, everything else in my life had gone from bad to worse. And if I kept lying to Ginny, that friendship would end up fizzling too.

"You know, I heard that the speaker, Dr. Singh also wrote a book. He studied at Yale. His father was a farmer from Punjab. You see, *beta*, anything is possible if you put your mind to it," Daddy said, handing me the tiffin.

"*Hanji.*" I nodded, only half listening, and grabbed my bag. As I stood on the porch for a moment to readjust my backpack, a slight breeze brushed across my face, loosening a strand of frizz from my clip, but I didn't care. I let my hair flap freely. Dadima had once told me that the wind is God whispering to us and we should be still and listen. So I did.

I let the wind take my worries and questions and scatter them like dandelion fluff. I had no idea what God was telling me, but at least he still tried to talk to me. And maybe going to the "Your Karma, Your Life" talk was how I'd be able to figure out what he was saying.

The bus kids rushed down the hallway behind me. The past few days I'd timed my arrival to be a couple of minutes early so I wouldn't have to walk past the pillar and wonder if Sara would or wouldn't be waiting for me. Even though I knew she wouldn't be waiting, there was a tiny, almost invisible, part of me that hoped she might.

At least Ginny's locker was next to mine so I didn't have to stand alone and watch Lacy and Sara be all buddy-buddy every morning. I wanted to ask Ginny how her recycling club posters turned out, but she wasn't at her locker. She'd left our classroom at the bus bell yesterday to make the posters in the art room.

Lacy's laugh filled the hallway, and I quickly shoved my books into my locker.

"Hands off, Tom. Everyone will get a piece of cake later. Well, everyone I like anyway."

I turned to see what they were doing just as Lacy gave Sara an exaggerated prissy face.

Kate and Emma giggled. Sara's neck turned a deep red. She ran past me toward the bathrooms, holding her books in one arm and tugging at her skirt with the other hand. I really shouldn't have cared. I should have let her go and deal with this alone like how she'd left me to deal with 'Stache Attack by myself since that day at the pool.

As much as I wanted to pretend I hadn't seen Sara run toward the bathroom, and as much as I wanted to go into the classroom and talk to Ginny about her recycling posters, I knew what I had to do.

Sara's sniffles were muffled behind the first stall door. I didn't even know if she'd ever actually been in a stall before. She'd always held her pee until she got back home.

I knocked lightly, my heart feeling like a scoop of ice cream right out of the freezer—softening slowly, with just the edges melted, but still hard and stiff in the middle.

"Sara, it's me," I said. "Are you okay?"

"No. I mean, yes. I'm fine."

"Please, Sara. Open up."

"Why? What do you want? To rub it in my face how everyone loves Lacy and no one likes me? Even you?"

"What? Look, Lacy exaggerates, that's all. I'm not friends with her."

The stall door swung open. Sara's hair fell out of a messy low ponytail, and pink rimmed her eyes. "Really? Because it sounded like you two were having a good time at your house yesterday."

"It's not like that."

"So she wasn't at your house?" Sara put her hand on her hip.

"She was. It's just that it was for school, not like I invited her over to hang out."

"For school? She said it was because you invited her."

I didn't want to say anything about Study Buddies, so I skipped over her question. "But why is she mad at you?"

"Because somehow she thinks I told everyone that she was held back."

"You did," I said.

"How do you know that?"

"I was in the bathroom that day . . ." The conversation was not going where it was supposed to. "I mean, I heard you, but I didn't say anything to Lacy."

"I can't believe this. Whose side are you on?"

Sara tried to push past me, but I blocked her way. She looked right into my eyes, and I almost moved aside. Instead I took a deep breath.

"I'm not taking sides. I've never defended Lacy, but you have. So why'd you tell Kate and Emma?"

"Sometimes I think people only want to be

friends with me because I hang around with Lacy. I just thought if I told Kate and Emma, they'd like me better. Maybe I'd seem cooler than Lacy." A tear rolled down Sara's cheek, but she quickly sniffed and pulled her hair over her shoulder.

"Yeah, but—"

Sara put her hand up to stop me. "You can stop pretending you're so perfect. It's not like you wouldn't have told if you knew. It's so obvious you can't stand her." With that, she shoved past me.

The thing is, I *did* know Lacy's secret and I didn't tell anyone. It was like Sara had forgotten what kind of person I was—what kind of people *we* were. Until she remembered, I didn't want to know her at all either.

As I put my tiffin in the storage closet, I noticed Lacy's cake on the shelf below my spot. The rectangular cake had frosting the same icy blue as her eyes. A yellow, flowered surfboard stuck out of the middle. There wasn't a number on the cake anywhere.

I scooted into my chair behind Ginny. "How'd your posters turn out?"

Ginny didn't turn around. She didn't even answer, not even with a shrug.

"Hey, Kar," Lacy said, walking up to my desk. "Did you see my cake? Isn't it cool?"

I guess now that Lacy knew it was Sara who'd told everyone about her being held back, she thought a piece of cake would make up for blaming me.

"The surfboard's exactly the same design as the one I had in California. My friends in surf club had it made for me when I moved, since I couldn't bring my real one here."

"Hmm." I stared at the back of Ginny's head and wished Lacy would leave already. If Lacy wanted to make things worse between Sara and me, I'd already done a good job of that in the bathroom. I didn't want her to come between Ginny and me too.

"I'll save you a piece. See you at lunch," she said, walking back to her seat.

I leaned forward and tapped Ginny on the back. "Do you need help putting up your posters during lunch?" I asked.

"I thought you just made plans for lunch," Ginny said without bothering to turn around.

"You don't really think—"

The bell rang, drowning out my explanation. Ginny ignored me all through two bells of English and our weekly health science class. Somehow she even managed to get out the door first and into math class before I could catch her.

When I settled in my seat in Mr. McKanna's class, I looked back to try to catch Ginny's eye, but she stared out the window.

David tripped into the room. When he sat in his seat, his waist pack squished against the desk. Poor Scooter. I glanced over at Ginny, but her eyes hadn't moved from the window.

Mr. McKanna was absent, so we had a sub. She couldn't find the quizzes Mr. McKanna had left for us, even after asking Mrs. Clark to come in and help search for them. We sat and did worksheets instead, even though Derek begged for her to let us play math relays.

I finished my worksheets in ten minutes, so I just traced all my numbers again and again, wishing the bell would ring. I wanted to catch Ginny so I could help her with the posters and explain again that I didn't have any plans with Lacy.

I looked over my shoulder, again. David wiped his forehead and bounced his leg up and down. His eyes darted around the room at the slightest noise or shuffle of paper. Something was definitely up with him today. He was acting so much weirder than usual.

The sub asked for a volunteer to collect all the papers, and Ginny's hand shot up. I tried to linger, but I got pushed out of the room with the rest of the class. Everyone was eager to get to lunch.

I put my books under my homeroom desk and followed Lacy to the storage closet to get my lunch. I'd wait around for Ginny to get her posters and talk to her then.

Lacy opened the storage closet door and screamed. "Ewww! Ew, ew, eeuuuuwwww."

Derek and Tom pushed their way past me. The rest of the class ran behind them and shoved each other to get a better look in the storage closet.

"Whoa!" Tom yelled.

"Man, looks like somebody hurled in here!" Derek said with a laugh.

"Karma! What did you do?" Lacy yelled, fighting back a strangled sob.

A strange quiet fell over the room. All eyes landed on me.

My throat throbbed, but I couldn't swallow.

"Massive 'Stache Attack!" Derek said, raising his hand to give me a high five.

I kept my hands at my side and inched toward the storage closet, afraid to know what I'd see.

"That is totally 'Stache, Karma." Tom patted my back and pushed me forward until I stood face-to-face with Lacy.

Behind her an infamous yellow-brown mush covered the floor of the storage closet. Speckles of white and blue cake frosting and chunks of vanilla cake floated in the dal.

The food from my tiffin and Lacy's cake were a messy goo all over the floor. The shelf my lunch had been on looked kind of wobbly. I stepped closer to give it a shake, but stopped.

Just when I thought it couldn't get any worse, it did.

Ginny's posters.

I moved in front of the door and turned, searching for a sign that Ginny had come into the classroom. The class moved and let her through. Her eyes went first to me and then over my shoulder.

"You did this. I know you did," Lacy said to me.

I couldn't tear my eyes away from Ginny as she took in the mess of what the cake and dal had done to her posters, which were now soaked and ruined.

I shook my head, trying to focus. Ginny's mouth hung open, and her shoulders fell.

"I didn't— I wasn't— I— The shelf is wobbly—" I stuttered.

"Save it, " Lacy said as she pushed past me. "I'm getting Ms. Hillary."

Murmurs rippled through the room. Everyone, even Ginny, took two steps back, leaving a circle of space around me. I didn't know what to do. I searched for a pair of eyes that might be nice and believe me, but the minute mine met anyone's, the person quickly looked away and started to whisper to the person next to them.

Ms. Hillary rushed into the room, followed by Lacy.

"She ruined it. She ruined my cake, and the surfboard isn't there."

Ms. Hillary stood next to me and put one hand on Lacy's shoulder and the other on mine. "Okay, off to lunch," she said to the rest of the class. "I just need to have a word with Karma and Lacy. The rest of you, hurry up. Derek, when you pass the office, can you please inform the office that we need a janitor in here?"

Derek nodded seriously, but when Ms. Hillary turned back to Lacy and me, he gave me a 'Stache Attack with a thumbs-up.

Before Ms. Hillary could say anything, Lacy said, "She pushed my cake over and then tried to cover it up by dumping her own lunch. The surfboard was a going-away gift from my friends. My *real* friends."

"Girls. Maybe we should go to the office to sort this out."

My back stiffened at the word "office." Lacy lifted her chin like it was what she'd wanted the whole time. Well, at this point nothing surprised me. My karma had gone from bad to worse to unbelievably and insanely terrible.

I sat in the office, staring at my hands. A swirl of thoughts and feelings traveled down to my stomach, making me glad I didn't have my dal to eat for lunch.

The red plastic chair dug into my shoulder blades as I rested my head against the wall and closed my eyes.

Ms. Hillary had taken Lacy into the counselor's office to call her mom and explain what had happened, not that anybody really knew what had happened. The whole class had been together all morning. I couldn't think of a single person who would have wanted to ruin Lacy's cake, Ginny's posters, or my lunch. It didn't make any sense.

The office door swung open. It was David. A very disheveled David. He wiped at his forehead with the back of his hand and pushed through the nurse's door.

"Karma," Ms. Hillary said, walking toward me. "I just got off the phone with Lacy's mom. I'm still not sure what happened with the cake, but Lacy's mom wasn't too worried. I assured her there had been some kind of accident. Lacy has asked to go home. Would you like to do the same?"

Daddy would have a massive heart attack if he had to come pick me up after having to get Kiran on the first day of school. I shook my head.

I'd rather Daddy not know anything about what had happened. Then, after the talk at the gurdwara tonight, I'd be able to fix everything and Daddy would never have to know.

Chapter Twenty-Four

The rest of the school day was basically me avoiding everyone and everyone mostly glaring at me, except for a few 'Stache Attacks thrown my way.

At home, as I got dressed in my Punjabi suit, I tried to imagine I was covering up the me that everyone at school blamed for ruining Lacy's cake, to make a new and improved version of myself.

It was pretty easy to do in my favorite suit. The bottoms were turquoise, with an embroidered pattern of silver and red beads from my knees to my ankles. The top had similar designs down the front, and the sheer turquoise of my *chunni* had matching beads at the edges.

Daddy whistled as he came down the stairs, his

beard smooth and tucked into his turban. I rested the *chunni* on my shoulders because I wouldn't need to cover my head until we arrived at the talk.

In the car, Daddy kept the music quiet. In bigger cities the Sikh gurdwara actually looked like a church-type building, but the one in Creekview was a house that'd been converted into a temple. Only the flags out front let you know it wasn't a regular house. Most people probably didn't realize it existed, even with the flags. I pulled my *chunni* up to cover my head as Daddy parked the car.

We took off our shoes and entered the *langar*, where they served a free meal to anyone who came in, that took up the entire downstairs. Upstairs was divided into the *darbar*, where we worshiped, and a couple of classrooms.

Dr. Gurwinder Singh's lecture would be held downstairs in the *langar* to accommodate the crowd of mostly college-age boys and girls and a couple of older men and women. No one else my age had come.

Daddy helped some other men bring a podium to the front of the room, and Dr. Singh began his talk.

I pulled out my notebook and bit the end of my

pen. I was ready. Ready to be told all the answers to end this cycle of bad karma, to finally get rid of my mustache and hopefully get Ginny and maybe even Sara back as friends. I held my breath as Dr. Singh opened his mouth and began to speak.

"There are no answers, my friends. We are all endlessly searching for the truth, and there is no end to our searching. No end to seeking answers. One hand drives everything, as Gurbani says, so our seeking is futile. Your karma is driven by the hand of One." He held up his pointer finger and paused. "What can we do?"

Another dramatic pause.

I waited, at the edge of my seat, pen poised to scribble the Answer.

"Nothing."

That is exactly what he said.

Nothing.

It was like someone promised you an apple pie but gave you an old apple instead. I'd been waiting so long for this moment that I could taste it. But instead of the satisfying mouthful of pie, I got a rotten apple with a worm in it.

I dropped my pen onto my lap, too stunned to

absorb what else he rattled on and on about for the next hour.

"Wasn't that insightful? So profound," Daddy said as he opened the still groaning car door for me.

I wadded my *chunni* between my hands and squeezed as we pulled out of the parking lot and onto the main road.

"*Beta*, I'm so glad you suggested we go." Daddy drummed the steering wheel.

"I don't get it."

"Well, parts of it were quite deep—"

"No, Daddy. I don't get it. Everything. What's the point? If nothing I do will change anything, then why do I even try?"

"*Beta*, is that all you heard? You must understand that Dr. Singh was making a point. There are things that as a human we can't control. Ultimately God decides. He chooses. But if we are faithful, all will be well."

"How did you hear that? He said it's futile. There's no hope!" My voice cracked.

"You know, *beta*," Daddy said, slowing to a stop at a traffic light, "sometimes things seem hopeless and we feel powerless, but we're never alone. You have family and friends, and most importantly, you have God. Dr. Singh was just being honest. We will never have all the answers. If we had all the answers, we'd be God. It wasn't meant to upset you. It should spur you to focus on what is important, rather than on things that don't matter."

Maybe I was supposed to believe that my mustache wasn't a big deal, that it was trivial. That having a mustache wouldn't matter when I grew old. But it *did* matter.

"I didn't realize this talk meant so much to you, Karma. Maybe I'm not the best at this kind of stuff, but do you remember that story your dadima used to tell?" Daddy drove slowly through the intersection. "About the lump of clay and the potter?"

I nodded, sitting back in the seat, wanting to take the words of this familiar story and wrap them around me.

"The potter had a lump of clay and started to knead it. The kneading felt good, like a massage. But as the potter worked longer and harder, the clay started to protest. 'Ouch, you're hurting me. Please stop!' The potter reassured the clay but kept kneading. Then he put the clay on the wheel and began to spin it, cupping it in his hands with a gentle grip. The clay relaxed into the potter's hands, but the spinning got faster and faster, and he called out again, 'I'm so dizzy. Please stop!' But the potter kept spinning, promising the clay it was in good hands. Then the potter placed the clay into a hot kiln. The intense heat was too much for the clay. It protested again, 'It's too hot. Please stop!' The potter continued, but with tears in his eyes. He waited for the correct amount of time before he took the clay out, and then he began to paint the clay. The clay liked the cool paint and the smooth bristles and relaxed, but soon the brush began to tickle. 'It tickles,' the clay laughed. 'Please stop!' The potter said to be patient and continued to work until the paint was just right. Then he put the clay back into the kiln. The clay was too weary to protest. The kiln was just as hot as before, and finally he yelled in protest, 'It's too hot. Please stop!' When it was time, the potter brought the clay out and put it on a table. It was the most beautiful, perfectly formed vase with glossy paint. And do you know why the potter couldn't stop when the clay asked him to?"

I nodded. "Because the clay would have cracked

and it never would have turned into a vase," I whispered.

"*Hanji.* Sometimes God lets bad things happen to us, because if life was so easy, why would we seek him? We'd all rely on ourselves and never be stretched."

We pulled into the parking lot of the Ice Cream Parlor, an old-fashioned ice cream place. The red and white lights from the sign reflected off the car windows. I traced the letters with my eyes and willed my eyes to stay dry.

Dadima had told me the potter and clay story many times before, but it'd just been a story without any real meaning. Today the pain of that clay meant something to me. I'd been squeezed and burned. I knew how it felt to be that piece of clay, being flung around and nobody really paying attention to what the clay wanted. Everyone in my class thought I'd ruined Lacy's cake. Ginny thought I'd lied about Lacy and that I'd ruined her posters. And I'd lost Sara for good. The difference between the piece of clay in the story and me was that I hadn't turned into a vase. I was still hairy, unsure me.

I really wished Dadima were here to tell me the story. She always knew how to explain things to me.

She made me feel sparkling and hopeful, like I could reflect everything bad and negative off me.

"*Beta*, I know you miss Dadima and I know it would be easier for you to have your mom around more, but if there's anything—"

"Thanks, Daddy," I said to cut him off then, because I didn't want to talk about my mustache or for Daddy to think he had to say anything else. I said, "So, ice cream?"

Daddy smiled, his face softening in relief. "That's why we're here."

I tossed my *chunni* onto the seat of the car as I got out.

Inside the Ice Cream Parlor, I inhaled the sugary air that filled the place. It had smelled the same since I'd come here after my first day at kindergarten. Watching the lady scoop the ice cream into the frosted glass dish and pour thick, fudgy sauce on top softened the hard shell of hopelessness that had formed around me. I asked for an extra cherry. The lady winked at me and added three.

I couldn't even wait till we sat down. I took the first bite as Daddy paid. I turned around and saw Tom sitting at a table with an older boy and two adults that must have been his parents. The man had the same nose, and the woman shared Tom's hair color. He nodded and half waved at me.

I blinked and slowly took the spoon out of my mouth. Tom looked so quiet and shy sitting with his family. I knew I was gaping, but I couldn't understand Tom in this new way—without Derek, without school. It was too long a pause between his wave and my reaction.

My face heated up as I remembered that I was wearing a Punjabi suit. Maybe Tom's smile was a smirk. The older boy, who must have been his brother, nudged him and said something, making Tom turn red and punch the boy in the arm.

"Shall we sit down?" Daddy asked.

His voice echoed off the tile floor and the absurdly high ceilings. I walked to the corner furthest from Tom and his family. Daddy slurped his milk shake and bounced his knee while I played with the hot fudge sauce on my spoon. I took a few bites, but it tasted too sweet.

"*Beta*, you've got something . . ." Daddy reached toward my face and wiped at my upper lip. His hand shot back like he'd been bit. The realization of what had happened hit me about three seconds after it hit Daddy. He'd jerked his hand back because he'd realized it wasn't hot fudge sauce.

It was a mustache.

Dr. Gurwinder Singh was right—life was hopeless.

Chapter Twenty-Five

Even in the darkness of my room, the embarrassment burn and fury of Daddy finally noticing my mustache rushed through my veins in choppy surges, like Daddy pulsing tomatoes, onions, and spices in the blender for a curry.

I waited until silence filled the house and the floorboards were still and settled in their places, like they were snuggled in bed. The only noises now were a low murmur of music that pulsed under Kiran's door, and Daddy's snores spluttering from his bedroom.

I tiptoed across the hall to the bathroom and inched the door closed so the *click* would be more of a slide and less of a *pop*. I didn't bother locking it, afraid doing so would be too loud. I paused and waited for any noise or movements.

Nothing changed. They were all deep in sleep. I allowed myself to exhale, but I didn't relax for long. I had a mission.

My plan went against Dadima's belief that a proper Sikh didn't cut their hair. I could still picture Dadima's legs and how the hair on them peeked out at the bottoms of her Punjabi suit pants. She even had little clusters of hair on her big toes. But I also remember finding a thread in her hair and asking if she'd been sewing something. She'd blushed a light pink, and Mom had later told me that she had been threading her eyebrows but hadn't wanted to admit to removing hair.

If Dadima threaded her eyebrows, then shaving my mustache couldn't be that big a deal. Plus, Dr. Singh had said that nothing I did mattered.

Mom kept her razor on the side of the bathtub with a can of creamy foam. I wasn't sure if it was necessary to use the stuff, so I decided against it. The pipes in our house groaned and whined, so I thought it better to do this without any water.

I grabbed the pink razor. The handle sat softly in my fingers like it should fit naturally in my palm. It didn't. My hand shook.

I took a deep breath and leaned toward the

mirror, so close that my nose nearly touched. This time I wanted to get a good look at the hair and figure out the best way to shave it. I wasn't sure if I should go up or down with the razor. I didn't know if I should start with my face or somewhere else that I could hide if I needed to, like maybe my legs or arms.

No, I'd do my face. It was the smallest area of hair, and it couldn't be that bad.

I grasped the razor tightly in my right hand. I held it just above my lip and decided that I'd shave down. Start at my nose and stop at my lip. I repeated it in my head—nose, down, lip. Nose, down, lip.

Okay, I told myself, *this is it. No big deal. Nice and easy.* I closed my eyes, which I knew was really stupid, but I couldn't bear to watch myself. I opened them as soon as the razor brushed the top of my lip, but I didn't move the pink razor right away.

I closed my eyes again and lifted the razor off my face. I slowly opened my eyes so I could inspect what I'd done.

It was gone!

I only had half a mustache. I stared at myself in the mirror. It had worked! I did the other side the same way but kept my eyes open.

My mustache was gone. My body tingled with satisfaction. I thought of walking into school and seeing everyone's reaction.

All the "Wow, you look great, Karma!" "You look so nice today," "There's something so mature about you," comments.

I reached up to rub the smooth skin above my lip. The hairs on my arms seemed so bushy with my mustache gone. Shaving my arms and legs couldn't be any worse than what I'd just done.

I closed the lid of the toilet seat and put my leg up. After resting the razor next to my ankle, I pulled up toward my knee. It went smoothly for the first third of my leg. Then it kind of got stuck. A handful of fuzz clogged the razor, so I got a tissue to wipe it off. But all I managed to do was shred the tissue and cut my finger.

I reached for more tissues, and the hair that had been stuck to the razor fell in clumps to the floor. When I walked to the sink to shake off the hair from the razor, the floor felt gritty under my feet. I lifted up my foot to look at the bottom of it. Hundreds of black hairs stuck to my heel. The bathroom had become a real mess.

I'd never realized how messy this whole shaving

thing could be. It never looked that way in commercials. Maybe if I used water, it would be less messy. I tried to keep the water at a slow, steady stream, but that made the pipes whine and gurgle, so I had to turn it up more to make the pipes be quiet.

When I had finally managed to get one leg mostly shaved, my face started to burn. I ignored it and decided to focus on my other leg. I shook the razor over the sink, and most of the hair fell off. I had to keep stopping and shaking the razor. It was a slow and annoying job. Especially now that clumps of hair were clogging the sink and more clumps had fallen onto the bathroom floor around the toilet.

My legs started to burn the same as my face. I looked into the mirror. Little red dots spotted my face, and a few started sprouting on my legs, too. My knees were covered in cuts, and I'd missed an entire strip of hair down my right shin.

Maybe this hadn't been such a good idea after all. I filled a cup with water and moved toward the bathtub. I poured the water down my right leg so that I could shave the missed strip. The razor went smoothly over the water but then dug into my skin.

The skin turned completely white. Then, just as quickly as it had turned white, little beads of red leaked through, and before I knew it, blood ran halfway down my shin.

I grabbed as many tissues as I could and started dabbing at the blood. It soaked through the tissues in a matter of seconds. I tried to wet the tissues, but the water mixed with the blood and dripped across the floor. I rushed over to get more tissues. Finally I got a whole wad of tissues. They stuck to the blood like magic. Gross, but magic.

I stood in the middle of the bathroom and stared at the mess I'd made. The sight of hair, shreds of tissues and toilet paper, and drips of blood littered all over the floor made me sweat. My skin still burned. I wiped my upper lip, and a red streak smeared across the back of my hand. I leaned closer to the mirror. The little beads of blood mingled with sweat over tiny red bumps where I'd shaved.

Did shaving give you pimples? I pulled at the skin above my lips and felt tears puddle behind my eyes as the rest of me filled with an anxious sense of dread. What had I done? There was nothing I could do now. It was worse than before I'd started.

My thoughts of being hairless and stunning as I walked into school on Monday vanished.

I turned around to start cleaning up. The blood-stained tissues fell off my leg in a heap. I grabbed them and tried to blot up the drips from the floor, just as the bathroom door creaked open.

Chapter Twenty-Six

I froze, standing with a wad of bloodied tissues in one hand. Daddy made a strangled yelp noise. "Karma! You're awake." He half covered his eyes and turned his back to me. "I was just going to . . ."

Everything else happened so fast, but somehow also so slowly and detailed too that every sound inside and outside my body echoed in my ears. A gurgle rose from my stomach, up into my throat, and choked out of my mouth. The floorboards moaned by the bathroom door just before Mom's face appeared beside Daddy's.

They both stared at the tissues wadded in my hand. I watched as they slowly took in the rest of the scene around me. The water coming in a slow steady stream from the sink faucet, the small piles of hair scattered all over the floor.

Mom pushed her way past Daddy into the bathroom and closed the door behind her.

"Go back to bed. I've got this." She turned to me and whispered, "Are you okay? Is it your period?"

"Mom!"

"What?" She cupped my face in her hands and turned it toward the light above the sink. "Why is your face bleeding?"

I pushed her hand off my face more forcefully than I'd meant to. "I'm fine. It's fine. I'll clean everything up." I bent down to grab some tissues. My eyes burned and everything went blurry. I started to cry. Not just a normal cry but the embarrassing, sobbing kind of crying when you can't even talk, you're too busy making sure you're getting enough oxygen to your brain.

Mom was a blurry outline through my tears, but I could tell from how her hand patted my back in short, stiff movements as she pulled me toward the edge of the tub to sit that she was surprised at my outburst. That made me cry even harder.

"Karma, do you want to tell me what this is all about?"

I shook my head, still heaving too much to form any words.

She nodded and rubbed my back in a circle. Her touch unhooked a calm in me that spread like thick syrup to all my limbs. A summer's worth of tears had poured out of me in just a few minutes, and all I wanted then was to climb under my comforter.

"Oh, sweets, you may think I don't understand what you're going through, but I do."

I wanted to scoff, but instead snot bubbled out of my nose. I lifted my chin so my eyes were level with her face. She scanned the bathroom. I couldn't tell if she was thinking about how much it needed a good cleaning or if she wished she were back in bed. I expected her to sigh and tell me to get some sleep, but she kept talking.

"Has someone been making fun of you or bothering you?" She reached for my chin so that I couldn't turn away.

I nodded.

"Brothers are like that. It's just what they do. But if you're uncomfortable with something— anything—you can talk to me."

We sat in silence, surrounded only by the soft sounds of our breathing.

"It's not Kiran. It's kids at school," I said as quickly and quietly as I could, hoping the words would get lost before they reached Mom's ears.

"Oh, sweetie."

Mom held me and let me cry big, silent tears that burned the top of my lip. "I've made it worse," I said between heaves. I would be a big lump of un-spun, un-formed, un-painted, and un-fired clay for the rest of my life.

"You haven't made anything worse or better. All you did was change something. You can change your clothes or your hair, but you can't change you."

I rolled my eyes and wiped my cheeks.

Mom handed me a tissue.

"I wish you'd asked me about shaving. I didn't even know it bothered you." Mom looked up at the ceiling. "I guess I knew something was wrong, but I really hoped you'd come to me, like before."

I nodded and blinked. A few big tears teetered off the edge of my eyelids when I did. "But things aren't the way they were before. You're never even here half the time."

"Oh, I know." She squeezed me closer to her again. "I really just thought it'd get easier, but I'm floundering around at work. Then I come home and I just don't know where I belong anymore. But, Karma, I'm never too busy for you or Kiran."

I twisted the soggy tissue in my hand and thought about that. None of us knew where we belonged right now. Kiran at high school, Daddy at home, Mom at work, and me, I didn't know where I fit in with Sara or Ginny or even my family.

"Growing up is so hard," Mom said, and sighed. "I know I'm busy, but I'm not blind. I should have said something. It's just that you usually come to me if something's going on. I never realized. I'm so, so sorry." She moved her hand from my shoulder and rubbed my back again. "You know, they make products for facial hair. Bleaches and small little razors that won't irritate your skin so much." She touched my face with both her hands. "But I don't want you to do anything unless it bothers *you*. Don't ever change because of what someone else says." Now *her* eyes were watery.

It felt nice to sit on the edge of the bathtub and soak up the reassurance and warmth that radiated from Mom. I didn't want it to end.

"Everyone notices it, Mom. Even Daddy."

"Oh, honey. I know it's uncomfortable, and

unfortunately, people will notice. They always will. Sometimes they'll make fun of you, sometimes they'll say mean things, but you do know that even if you shave it or wax it, you are still Karma Khullar. People notice what's on the outside before they try to find what's on the inside. That can hurt, or you can learn from this. Everyone has a mustache. Maybe not on their face, but everyone has something they try to hide or are embarrassed about."

"So I shouldn't try to get rid of it?"

"Well, that's up to you. Do you want to know what I think?"

I nodded. I wanted to know it was okay to not want a mustache.

"Girls shave their armpits and their legs. But if you want to get rid of the hair on your upper lip, I'll take you to get products meant for your face. There is nothing wrong with not wanting the hair. However"—she stopped and put her hand under my chin—"there is something wrong with making fun of others. Do you want me to call the school?"

I shook my head. "Not yet."

"Come on, then." Mom stood up and held out her hand. I let her lead me to my bed and tuck me in burrito-style just the way I liked.

She left my bedroom door open just enough and I waited until she clicked the bathroom light off before I closed my eyes. Even though I hadn't had a divine intervention at the temple, I knew the answer to my questions—and it wasn't nothing, as Dr. Singh had said. He might believe that hope in hopelessness made sense, but that was because men were supposed to walk around with hair on their faces.

Mom was right, I could shave, but it didn't really change anything. 'Stache Attack already existed out there in the wide-open world of Holly Creek Middle School. If I really wanted to change things with Ginny or Sara or Lacy, I had to turn "nothing" into "something."

Just as I felt myself nodding off to sleep, the idea of how to turn everything around came to me. Maybe a karma curse did exist, but Dr. Singh had said I couldn't do anything about it.

I'd show him.

Chapter Twenty-Seven

The smell of coffee and buttery pancakes filled the air when I woke up the next morning. I inhaled deeply, relieved that Mom would be home to help cool the embarrassment that would plague me every time I had to avoid Daddy's eyes. I grabbed the note I'd scribbled last night and reread it to make sure it still sounded like a good idea.

It did.

"Morning, darling," Mom said as I shuffled into the kitchen. "The boys are busy in the study and don't want to be disturbed all day."

The closed door to the study was a relief. I could delay the embarrassment for that much longer.

"I thought it'd be a good idea to do some shopping today. Just the two of us," Mom said, sliding a stack of steamy pancakes across the counter to me.

"Actually, I have a couple of things I need to get while we're out," I said, trying to get a grasp on my plan.

"Good. We'll stop at the pharmacy too if you want."

A warmness radiated from my neck to behind my ears at the mention of the pharmacy. "Yeah, okay."

Shopping was tiring business even when it was with Mom and for things that were actually nice and what I wanted. I chose a dark blue corduroy skirt and a pair of tights. The good thing about the weather getting cooler was, I would be able to cover most of the hair on my body. As for my mustache, it was gone for now, but when I touched above my lip, my fingers ran over little pricks where the hair wanted to grow back.

After lunch we stopped at a pharmacy near my favorite used-book store. It was one of those big pharmacies that had everything from phones to a refrigerated section. I was glad Mom chose that pharmacy, because it was a good twenty minutes from our house and I wasn't likely to run into someone I knew. I said several silent thank-yous when she insisted to the man in the store that we didn't need any help.

Mom pulled a few things off the shelf. "This is a cream bleach specifically for your face. We should start with this. It'll lighten your hair but won't irritate your skin the same way shaving can." Then she grabbed a few razors that had a sketch of a woman using it on her cheeks and eyebrows.

Oh no. I didn't know you could get hair on your cheeks, too.

Mom must have picked up on the panic in my eyes, because she gave my arm a reassuring squeeze. "Don't worry. We'll practice using it together."

She added a family-size bag of strawberry Twizzlers to our things. "We'll hide them in my bag as we read next door." She winked.

"I need to grab a few things over by school supplies," I said.

"Take your time. I'm just going to browse."

Relieved that I could grab what I needed without having to explain to Mom what exactly I had planned, I headed over to the school supplies.

Holding several pieces of different-colored poster board, a box of markers, and a package of rainbow-colored glitter glue in my arms filled me with a nervous excitement, making me want to rush home and get started on my plan right away.

I pretended to read my new book on the ride home. Things had been so strained at home before I'd told Mom about my mustache, and I didn't want to break the nice pillowy quiet that surrounded us now. I felt comfortable and wanted to settle into it.

When we walked through the door, folksy guitar music blared from Daddy's study. I put my bags on the dining table and checked the laundry baskets out of habit. They were empty. Daddy really had started to get the hang of this staying-home thing.

"Mary! Karmajeet! Come in here," Daddy called.

I poked my head into the study. *"Hanji?"*

Not a sight I was used to seeing—Daddy and Kiran working together on the computer. Daddy hardly let anyone sit in his chair, much less tell him how to do something.

"Look what we've created!" Daddy turned his computer so I could take in the whole monitor.

A mad-scientist-looking cartoon wearing a turban was waving a wand at the top of a page that said *Your Science Guru.*

"No, no, no," Daddy said. "I want these letters to

be shaded in the back, and it should be all capitals. 'YOUR SCIENCE GURU,' all caps," Daddy said.

Kiran's fingers started to dart across the keyboard. "Do you see how I have to type this and then—"

"That's what I did," Daddy snapped.

"No. Actually, your code—"

"Doesn't matter." Daddy stopped and watched Kiran type for a moment. "You really do have a knack for this computer stuff, don't you?"

Kiran shrugged, but I knew it meant so much more than Kiran let on.

"The cartoon and title were Kiran's ideas. It's great, huh?" Daddy asked.

"Yeah. It's good," I said.

"Why are you yelling?" Mom asked, walking into the study behind us. "What is playing?" Mom asked.

"Did you know your son could play the guitar like that?" Daddy asked.

"That's you?" I asked Kiran.

"Well, it's a couple of us from band at school. We got permission to use some recording equipment."

"I'm impressed," Mom said.

"Yeah, me too," I said. Everyone had a smile on their face—even if Kiran's was more of a smirk.

"Should we add my guitar music to the page?" Kiran asked.

"How about Bollywood tunes?" Daddy asked.

"No way!" Kiran and I said together.

"Hey, this is my page," Daddy said.

"Half your page," Kiran said. "Besides, if you don't understand how to write the program, you can't choose the music." Kiran clicked away at a new code.

"Well, should I get some pasta started?" Mom asked.

"Pasta?" Daddy said, faking a gag. "There's chana masala in the fridge. I'll start some rice." He turned to Kiran. "And I insist that you put in the Bollywood music."

Dr. Singh had said that the hand of God drives everything. I pictured Babaji with massive puppeteer hands, moving everyone in the world. Dr. Singh's words scrolled across my mind like the highlights at the bottom of the news channel.

One hand drives everything. There are no answers. What can we do? Nothing.

I didn't agree with that. We *could* do something. Daddy had opened his door and let Kiran in. That was something and it was a start. I couldn't wait to get started on *my* something.

Chapter Twenty-Eight

Marker smudges and glitter stained the sides of my hands, but I'd finished all the posters. Once I'd started decorating, more and more ideas had come to me. I'd written them down before I'd gotten too scared. It felt bold to write things with marker and not be able to erase it.

Before bed Mom mixed some powder and cream together from the box of cream bleach we'd bought at the pharmacy. I tried to hold my breath as she spread it above my lip with a tiny spatula thing that came inside the box. The cream was cold on my skin but burned and tingled my nose worse than Daddy slicing onions. It bubbled and popped against my skin, but nothing moved or changed as I watched it in the mirror for the entire fifteen minutes.

After Mom wiped it off with a warm washcloth, my skin was too red to tell if it'd done much good. I blew on it, trying to get the tingle off my skin and out of my nose.

"All right, it's past your bedtime," Mom said. She followed me into my room and sat on my bed next to me.

I turned off the lamp and rolled toward Mom.

"Making those posters to help your friend's after-school group shows that you're really becoming a wonderful young lady," she said.

I rolled my eyes. I hated that phrase "young lady," but I let myself smile because it was dark in my room, too dark for my expression to be visible. The darkness also made me feel like I could say anything.

"Everything has been so different this year."

"Change isn't always a bad thing, you know," Mom whispered into my ear as she gave my ponytail one final brush with her fingers.

I wanted to believe that things did change for the better, that they would finally work out for me.

Daddy pushed a perfectly golden paratha across the counter to me. I watched as he chopped and sliced the vegetables on the cutting board. He'd actually gotten really good with the knife. The slices of onion were thin and even, not chunky the way they'd been a few weeks ago.

Mom rushed into the kitchen and gave Daddy and me a quick kiss. She grabbed the coffee that Daddy had already poured into a thermos for her.

Maybe Mom was right, all this change wasn't such a bad thing. I mean, Mom came home tired, but I knew she enjoyed working at the university, doing what she loved, and Daddy had never intended to be home, but if his knife skills were proof, it might actually be growing on him.

Daddy handed me a brown bag as I finished my paratha.

Confused, I opened it. Inside was a sandwich, applesauce, carrot sticks, and two cookies. "What's this?" I asked.

"Your lunch," Daddy said, turning back to the onions he'd dumped into the pan.

"Then what are you making?" I couldn't believe it. Now that he was giving me a normal lunch, all I wanted was my tiffin.

"Saag."

"Will it be done before school?" I asked.

"Should be. Why?"

"I'd rather take that than this bland junk," I said, holding up the brown paper bag.

Daddy put down the wooden spoon and turned to me. A laugh rolled out of his mouth and smoothed the deep lines across his face.

Without any thought I rushed toward him and hugged him around his middle. I felt like a little kid hugging him, but I also felt bigger, or maybe just older.

Daddy and Kiran helped me roll up the posters, and we drove to school together. Rain poured down outside. I didn't know if rain was a bad omen, so I told myself it was a good one because it had gotten me a ride to school. Plus, it was nice to think of the rain rushing the bad summer down the drains, making way for the good stuff that would happen. I clutched my tiffin and the plastic bag with the posters and sticky tack so I could put them up in the hallway.

The parking lot was only half full because I'd arrived a half hour before the buses. Daddy dropped me by the pillar Sara and I chose on orientation day to be our meeting spot. Maybe it was another bad omen, or maybe it was just a sign that things change but really they stay the same. That pillar was still there. It would still be there when I left Holly Creek Middle in a couple of years. Only Sara and I had changed.

I clung to Mom's words that change was a good thing and walked toward the sixth-grade wing to complete my plan.

Ms. Hillary wasn't in the classroom, so I peeked into Mr. McKanna's room.

"Morning, Karma. What brings you to school so early?" he asked.

"Um. Mr. McKanna. I wanted to know if it was okay to put up some posters for Ginny's recycling club."

"Of course. You need any help?" he asked.

"Thanks, I've got it." I wasn't sure I was ready for anyone's reaction just yet. I'd rather wait for the only reaction I cared about—Ginny's.

The bus kids started to pour in just as I shoved the last of my things into my locker. I clenched my jaw and fought the urge to run up and down the halls ripping down every poster I'd put up. I stared hard into my locker, waiting for anyone to notice them. So far the noises sounded normal.

Clutching my tiffin and books, I turned and headed to the classroom.

Then came the first reaction. Tom yelled, "The 'Stache-a-nator strikes back!"

"Ha! That's totally hilarious," Derek chimed in.

I could never tell if they were making fun of me or complimenting me. Today and from now on I chose to take it as a compliment, and I didn't bother to turn around. I walked into the classroom with my head high and full of hope.

I put my books under my desk and turned to find Ginny rushing into the classroom. Her hair was spritzed with raindrops, and her skin still radiated cold from the outside.

"Bold, Karma. That was bold." She walked up to me and hugged me tight. I laughed and hugged her with my free arm, the other still clutching my tiffin.

Then she pulled back. "'Don't Be 'Stache, Recycle Your Trash!' That's so brilliant." She shook her head, still grinning. "Everyone's talking about it."

"Well, I have to give Tom and Derek credit for coming up with the whole 'Stache thing."

Ginny shoved my arm. "Whatever. Everyone is going to want to recycle now. We can put mustaches on the recycle bins."

"Listen, Ginny. About Lacy. I never had plans with her. Well, I did, but it wasn't like that. I've been helping her in math, but she didn't want anyone to know." It sounded so stupid now that I said it.

"I didn't think you'd actually be friends with her, but I saw her leave with you that day when I was in the art room. I don't know. I guess I just thought after I'd told you about Derek and stuff, maybe you didn't really want to be friends."

I shook my head. "I still want to be friends."

"Duh," Ginny said with a laugh. "Anyone who makes posters like that is a real friend."

The early bell rang, and Ginny shoved her stuff under her desk.

"Where's Ms. Hillary?" I asked, noticing she wasn't hovering like normal.

Ginny shrugged. "Probably putting the last-minute touches on another superfun 'enriching' lesson."

We laughed, and Ginny walked with me to the storage closet. I almost dropped my tiffin when I saw what was on the floor inside.

"Oh no." I fell to my knees, putting the tiffin on the ground next to me.

Ginny gasped. "Is that . . ."

I nodded. Scooter lay on the floor of the storage closet with a chewed-up yellow surfboard next to him like he'd had a major wipeout. His chest wasn't moving, and the closet kind of smelled funny, like gym socks and mildew. He was dead.

There was a scream from behind us. Emma squealed, "Rat!" and the class erupted in chaos.

"Hey, isn't that from Lacy's cake?" Ginny said, pointing at the doll-size surfboard.

I cupped Scooter into my hands and wiped off the gnawed yellow plastic crumbs that were on his fur. It seemed the right thing to do even if it grossed me out. I mean, bubonic plague and all.

"Girls!" Ms. Hillary gasped as she clomped into the room, David's familiar shuffle close behind her. "The bell will— Oh my goodness."

"Scooter!" David's screech was buried under the commotion in the classroom.

"Calm down! Calm down!" Ms. Hillary yelled over all the noise.

David pushed my shoulder back to get at Scooter.

He scooped Scooter into his hands and held him to his nose.

"Is this Scooter?" Ms. Hillary asked.

Ginny and I turned to Ms. Hillary. She knew about Scooter?

"Oh, David." Ms. Hillary rushed to his side and patted his shoulder. "Karma, can you find an empty box on one of the shelves, please?"

Ginny and I both stood up and rummaged the shelves until we found two half-full boxes of paper and put all the paper into one box. We handed the empty box to Ms. Hillary. She took Scooter from David's hands and placed him gently in the box.

I couldn't believe how gentle Ms. Hillary was with Scooter. It was a whole new side of her.

The rest of the class had climbed off their chairs and were huddled around the storage closet.

"Well, class," Ms. Hillary said, still sitting on the floor next to David as he clutched the box to his chest, "I'm afraid there has been a grave injustice done."

Everyone nodded. I thought she was talking about the death of an innocent gerbil, but she turned her eyes toward me.

"Karma, it seems that Scooter escaped on Friday, and the entire mess with Lacy's cake can be explained by his disappearance."

The tiffin. The cake. The ruined posters. The chewed-up surfboard. The wobbly shelf. It was all caused by Scooter? I thought about him being scrunched up in David's waist pack all day, being fed through a tiny opening in the zipper. Poor thing must have been wanting out for a while. And on Friday, David had been so anxious.

"Sorry, Karma," David said, his shoulders still shaking. "I wanted to tell you . . ."

"It's okay." I reached over and patted his hunched back. It was hard to be mad at David or Scooter. David had only been trying to protect Scooter, and Scooter—well, he was a gerbil, and he probably just wanted a taste of freedom—and cake.

I stood up as Ms. Hillary guided David to her desk, and most of the class followed. A hand rested on my shoulder. I turned, expecting Ginny, but it was Sara. I wanted to pull away and ignore her, just like she'd done to me ever since Lacy had come to the pool with her that day.

"I can't believe David had a gerbil at school this whole time. I had no idea."

"Yep." It stung that she only believed Lacy's cake disaster wasn't my fault now because Ms. Hillary had explained what had happened.

Ginny looked up from David's side and smiled. Her eyes flicked to Sara, and her smile faltered slightly.

"Listen, Karma," Sara said, keeping her hand on my shoulder. "I'm really sorry. About everything. I really am."

I laughed—half scoff, half real. On the one hand it was a relief to hear Sara say sorry, but on the other, her sorry came after we'd found Scooter dead and Lacy had dropped her as a friend.

I opened my mouth to tell her that, but the sharpness of my thoughts smoothed as they reached my mouth. Then I noticed her chipped nail polish and how she'd traded her skirt for a pair of jeans today. Sara wasn't old Sara anymore, but she wasn't exactly new Sara either. She was Sara-here-and-now.

"I'm sorry too," I said. "I haven't really been myself. Well, actually I have been, but I don't want to be. I mean, I don't want to be jealous. And I think it's a good idea to have other friends." My eyes searched for Ginny, who was with the rest of the class hovering around Ms. Hillary's desk. Ginny stood at David's side, her arm around him as he told everyone about Scooter.

"I never meant to leave you like that," Sara said. "I wanted to be friends with Lacy, but I still wanted to be friends with you. Then it just got really confusing. That day in the bathroom, I wanted to make up, but I guess I was just too mad. Not really at you, more at myself. I actually dialed your house number that night but never pushed send. I don't know why."

This time my laugh came out 100 percent real. "I did the same thing the other day," I said, thinking of lying on my bed with the phone in my sweaty hands, wondering what in the world I'd say.

Sara grabbed me in a big hug. All the awkwardness was erased.

"Do over?" Sara asked.

That was Ruthie's way of getting out of trouble with their mom, by asking for a second chance. The reminder that our friendship went so deep that we didn't have to explain things to each other made talking with Sara fill me the way hot rice and dal filled me. It was a comforting, familiar sort of feeling that held with it memories and an understanding that no matter what changed, dal and rice always tasted the same.

Things weren't exactly the same as the old way, but I was learning to be comfortable in the newness.

Chapter Twenty-Nine

Lacy stood opposite me in the hallway, her arms crossed over her chest and her bottom lip hidden under her teeth. Ms. Hillary held the gnawed-on surfboard in her hand.

"Well, Lacy. It's obvious that Karma was not to blame for your cake on Friday," Ms. Hillary said. "Is there anything you want to say to Karma?"

It felt like kindergarten all over again.

"Sorry." Lacy cocked her head and flashed me a fake smile.

Ms. Hillary held the surfboard toward her.

"I'm not touching that thing," Lacy said, holding up her hands. "It's covered in gerbil slobber."

Ms. Hillary pulled a tissue out from her pocket and handed it to Lacy. Lacy grabbed the surfboard with the tissue but still held it away from her body.

"I hope this is all finally resolved?" Ms. Hillary said, raising her eyebrow at Lacy.

Lacy nodded.

"Follow me back to class, girls."

When Ms. Hillary turned, Lacy whispered, "Don't worry. You don't have to tutor me anymore. My mom found some old lady who used to teach high school. Thanks a lot."

She turned quickly and followed Ms. Hillary.

I couldn't believe that everything on Friday had been because of David's gerbil. Maybe it didn't have anything to do with my karma at all.

Wearing a jacket as I walked to school the next morning gave everything a sense of change. There was something fresh or even refreshing in the air.

I clutched the tiffin at my side and walked more slowly than normal because I wanted to enjoy the crisp air before it turned frigid in a couple of weeks and I'd have to wear a hat, scarf, and gloves. The buses were parked and unloading when I walked through the school gates.

Tom shoved past me, with Derek close behind.

"Sorry, 'Stache," Tom called without even slowing down.

I rolled my eyes. I still hated that nickname, but it didn't make my chest burn or my face heat up the same way it had at the beginning.

Ginny stood at her locker, putting her things away, when I walked up.

"Hey, morning. Did you hear Derek and Tom's newest?"

I shook my head and bit the inside of my cheek. Now what did they say about me? Okay, so maybe I lied. Maybe their insults still stung.

"Grandma Lacy."

"That's so stupid," I said.

"Tell me about it." Ginny reached into her locker and pulled out an envelope. "I got something for you. A little thank-you for helping out with the posters yesterday."

My cheeks warmed. I hadn't really helped. I'd ruined things and then just tried to repair it all. That wasn't the same thing. "Um."

"Just take it," Ginny said with a laugh.

"Thanks." I started to put it into my locker, not sure if Ginny wanted me to open it in front of her.

"Aren't you going to open it?" Ginny asked.

"Oh. Okay. Yeah, sure." I smiled and pushed my finger under the flap to rip it open. I pulled out a square bumper sticker that had the recycle triangle in green with the word "KARMA" in rainbow colors in the middle.

I held the sticker in both hands and stared at it. Ginny didn't know about the *Keep Calm and Hug Karma* bumper sticker Sara had given me. Ginny and I were still school friends for the most part. She hadn't been in my room or even to my house yet.

With new understanding, I traced my name surrounded by the recycle triangle. My eyes followed the arrows around and around the triangle. I'd been looking at this karma thing the wrong way the whole time. Even though I'd thought I'd been doing good by trying to get rid of the vices in my life, I hadn't gotten rid of any of my worries. Instead of good stuff going round and round, I'd been letting my worries get reused again and again until I was dizzy.

"If you don't like it . . . ," Ginny said, letting her voice trail off.

"No. I love it! Thanks." I hugged the bumper sticker to my chest. "Really. It's the best. You'll have to come over and see the bumper sticker Sara got me last year."

Ginny looked down at her books. "It's okay. If you want to be friends with her again, I get it."

"We can all be friends. Okay?"

Ginny nodded but still looked unsure.

I didn't blame her for being worried about Sara, but Dadima's favorite thing to do when Kiran or I complained about someone was to put one of our hands into hers. She'd turn it over and make us look at our hand from all angles.

"Are any of your fingers alike?" she'd ask.

I'd stare and try to find two fingers that looked almost alike, but I'd always end up shaking my head. None of my fingers were alike. Even my pointer and ring fingers were not alike, although they were close.

"No? Then how can you expect everyone in the world to be the same? Your hand would be useless without a thumb, and if it were all thumbs, it wouldn't function at all. You are how you are for a reason. It's part of a bigger picture we can't see because we're too small."

Sara wasn't the same as she had been last year, and I couldn't be sure we wouldn't get into another fight, but I was positive of how I felt right then—happy and not in the least bit worried.

"I'm serious. You should come over. Maybe this weekend?"

"That'd be cool," Ginny said.

I linked my arm through Ginny's. I couldn't wait to get home and put her bumper sticker on my mirror next to Sara's.

ACKNOWLEDGMENTS

You're holding this book because many, many people helped me. If your name isn't here, it's not because I forgot you—I'm saving you for the next book. ;)

Patricia Nelson, my agent, you took a chance on me, and your fierce belief in Karma has been unwavering. Thank you. Thanks also to the entire Marsal Lyon team for cheering Karma on.

Liz Kossnar, I've always felt in safe hands because you "get" it. xoxo

Beth Horner, you forced me to attend my first writer's conference and endured my first attempt at finishing a story.

Lisa, Sille, and Mille Thrane, you always asked me, "Is it done yet?" and now it is! Stefania Benedetti, your excitement: priceless.

Tina Boggars, you answered that e-mail and have remained gracious with your words and time ever since.

Shelley Sly, you've been an inspirational critique partner throughout the entire journey.

Richelle Morgan, you always read what I send and are famous for "pulling a Richelle," making me dig deeper. Michelle Leonard and Julie Artz, you both made Karma shine with your insights and critiques. And to all the Pennies at the Winged Pen: You are my people, and I'm better for knowing every one of you.

Brianna DuMont, you took time out of your busy schedule to sift through my tangled mess of words and find the passages that shone.

Melissa Nesbitt, you've been a voice of reason and sanity during "The Call" and every other step of this journey.

Thank you to the goddesses of contests: Brenda Drake for organizing and Summer Heacock for hosting Pitch Madness 2015. Green Team forever! Michelle Hauck and Amy Trueblood for hosting Sun vs. Snow and Ami Allen-Vath for mentoring and being the first to coin: #clubstache.

Fatim Jumabhoy and Fiona Hughes, you're the reason I have any sort of social life. Brandy Slavens, you always message me at just the right time and say it like it is. Elizabeth Slamka, you are my partner in crime. Don McKanna, you allowed me to use your name, and I have the best memories of your classes.

All the Wientges, but especially Nick, Pam, Nolan, and Autumn: Your love and enthusiasm sustain me.

ACKNOWLEDGMENTS

My children, you guys give me the desire to keep trying. My husband, you entertained my whims and answered all things Punjabi.

I thank my parents for never giving up on me and for all your years of prayers! Here it is! This is for you both.

Above all, I thank my Heavenly Father, who makes all things possible.

A Reading Group Guide to

Karma Khullar's Mustache

About the Book

As if starting middle school isn't scary enough on its own, Karma Khullar has to deal with a lot of other life changes at the same time. Her *dadima* has recently passed away, her father has become a stay-at-home dad, her mother has a new time-consuming job, and her best friend Sara wants to spend all her time with Lacy, her popular new neighbor. On top of all that, Karma has recently grown a mustache—seventeen black hairs, to be exact! She's nervous and self-conscious and isn't sure how she'll navigate her new life without her usual support network. Once school starts, it's up to Karma to figure out how to live up to her name and attract the good karma that she needs to survive sixth grade.

Discussion Questions

1. Why do you think Karma is so fixated on the emergence of her new mustache? Describe and discuss some of Karma's emotions associated with

the mustache. Is she overreacting? How would you react if you were her?

2. Karma's dad recently lost his job and has taken on a new role as a stay-at-home parent. Why do you think this is a hard adjustment for Karma? How do you think her dad feels about this new situation? How does his new role affect their relationship?

3. Compare and contrast the friendship between Sara and Karma and the friendship between Sara and Lacy. Why do you think Sara is drawn to Lacy when she moves to town?

4. When Karma feels that Sara doesn't care enough about her mustache she says, "a best friend should think *my* big deals were *her* big deals." What does Karma mean? Do you agree with her? Do you think that's an important part of a friendship?

5. Discuss Karma's relationship with Dadima. What were some of the important lessons that Dadima taught Karma and how did Karma apply those lessons to her life?

6. Karma's brother, Kiran, loves music, and their mother encourages his exploration of the arts. However, Karma's dad would prefer that he focus on the sciences. How do the arts differ from the sciences? Why do you think Karma's parents have different opinions on what's important? Do you think one is more important than the other?

7. Every day Karma brings her tiffin filled with Indian food to school. It's a source of both comfort and embarrassment for her. Discuss why it makes her feel these two very different emotions. Why do you think she chooses to continue bringing her tiffin to school at the end of the story?

8. Dadima taught Karma that the idea of karma is better explained by thinking "your actions start a trail of reactions" instead of thinking that "what goes around comes around." How are these two ways of looking at karma different from each other? Describe a time when your actions started a trail of reactions.

9. As Karma begins to keep track of her karma points, she has a list of vices to avoid, including

anger, pride, greed, and attachment to things of this world. Consider a time when you exhibited one of these vices. What happened? Is there anything you could have done differently to improve the situation and how you felt?

10. There are several instances in the book when Karma wishes Sara would stick up for her but Sara stays silent and ignores the situation. Karma says "until Sara had sat quietly around this past week, I never really got it that sometimes the silence hurts worse than the teasing." What does Karma mean by this? Do you agree or disagree?

11. When Karma goes to Lacy's house to tutor her, she discovers that Lacy and her mother are having a hard time adjusting to their new town. She also learns that Lacy was held back a year in school. How do you think Lacy's home life and being held back affect her behavior toward others?

12. Go back to chapter 24 and reread the story that Dadima told Karma about the potter and his lump of clay. Discuss the significance of this story and why it has suddenly become very meaningful to Karma.

13. When Karma's mom discovers her shaving in the bathroom, she admits to Karma that she's been preoccupied and regrets that Karma hadn't wanted to discuss her mustache with her. How does this represent a turning point in their relationship? What changes between them after their conversation?

14. At the end of the novel Karma says, "Things weren't exactly the same as the old way, but I was learning to be comfortable in the newness." What does she mean by this? Describe a time when you had to adjust to a new situation. Were you able to find comfort in the newness?

15. When Ginny gives Karma a bumper sticker with her name on it, Karma can't wait to go home and hang it next to the one from Sara. Why is this significant? How have Karma's thoughts on friendship shifted throughout the book?

16. How have the characters changed at the end of the novel? Who changed the most? What events do you think contributed to that character's progression?

17. Why do you think the author chose the name Karma for her narrator? How did the name Karma help shape the character?

18. Discuss an instance of peer pressure in the novel. Have you ever felt peer pressure to do something you didn't want to do? How did you react?

19. Throughout the novel, Karma is referred to as "Stache" and "Stache attack." Discuss some reasons why name-calling is very hurtful. Why do you think that some people resort to these hurtful tactics?

Extension Activities

1. In the novel, Karma decides to keep track of her "karma points." She would give herself points for not getting angry, prideful, greedy, or showing attachment to the things of this world. If she caught herself having any of these vices, she'd lose points. Try keeping track of your own karma points for one morning. How many points did you end up with? Is it difficult to avoid certain vices? Did you discover anything about yourself in this process?

2. When Karma goes to tutor Lacy for the first time, we read about the experience from Karma's point of view. Rewrite this scene from Lacy's point of view. Consider what Lacy would say about her mother's behavior and admission that Lacy was held back, how she would feel about having Karma over to her house, and how she would feel about needing a tutor.

3. Mrs. Clark suggests that each student come up with a big idea to put in the suggestion box. Come up with your own big idea for your class. Explain why your idea would be successful. Just like in the novel, your idea should be about making learning engaging beyond the classroom.

4. The food that Karma brings in her tiffin to school is unfamiliar to her classmates but it's very normal for Karma because it's part of her family's culture. Think of a food that represents your family's culture. Write about a memory you have that involves eating this food.

5. There are many instances of bullying throughout the novel. Brainstorm ways that you can help

prevent bullying in your school. Write a letter to your teacher presenting your ideas and explaining why bullying prevention is so important.

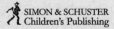

"Amina's anxieties are entirely relatable, but it's her sweet-hearted nature that makes her such a winning protagonist."
—*Entertainment Weekly*

★"A universal story of self-acceptance and the acceptance of others."
—*School Library Journal*, starred review

★"Written as beautifully as Amina's voice surely is, this compassionate, timely novel is highly recommended."
—*Booklist*, starred review

★"Amina's middle school woes and the universal themes running through the book transcend culture, race, and religion."
—*Kirkus Reviews*, starred review

"The wilder will teach the wolves how to be bold again, how to hunt and fight, and how to distrust humans. They teach them how to howl, because a wolf who cannot howl is like a human who cannot laugh."

"I loved the characters, the speed, the force of it all."
—PHILIP PULLMAN, author of *The Golden Compass*

ALL OF THE QUESTIONS.
ALL OF THE ANSWERS.

Judy Blume has a whole new look!
Which one will you read first?